I0556494

The Dragon's Blood Key

Book 1

The Legend of the Dragon's Blood Key

By

Linda L Barton

Copyright 2015©Linda L Barton

ISBN-10: 0692509224

ISBN-13: 978-0692509227

Dedication and Acknowledgments

I dedicate this book to my sweet grandchildren. Brianna, Syrea, Ralph, Arianna, and David, you each bring such joy into my life. Now grandma has written a book you can enjoy.

Editing, formatting, and cover design by

Deadly Reads Author Services

Dragon Image inside the book by Vectorolie

FreeDigitalPhotos.net

Chapter 1

Tales of the day when a Champion would come from a far-off realm filled the hearts of the people in the Kingdom of Walandra with hope. They had long awaited the one who wore the sacred Breast Plate and Blood Key to come and free them from the rule of the Evil Queen Alona.

For hundreds of years, Queen Alona had enjoyed complete rule over the Kingdom. Yet, she would soon find her rule challenged by the appearance of the Champion Abigail.

While wearing the sacred Breast Plate and Blood Key, which had transported Abigail to the realm of Walandra, she challenged Queen Alona in battle and fought without fear even as the Queen prepared to strike her down. Then at the last possible moment in a flash of blinding light, the Blood Key transported Abigail safely back to her realm. In a fit of rage, Queen Alona forbade the people of Walandra to speak the name of the Champion aloud again.

In spite of the Queen's demands, the subjects of the kingdom would regale the tale of the young woman who came to their world and fought the Evil Queen. They spoke in hushed tones, telling the story of Abigail, as they anxiously awaited her return to complete her destiny and save the kingdom.

Seventy years later…

"Why do we have to go? I want to stay home and hang out with my friends," Melissa moaned as she forced another pair of shorts into her overly stuffed suitcase.

"Stop your complaining. You'll have a good time, and besides, your father and I have wanted to get away alone for a long time," her mother chided.

Melissa rolled her eyes, not convinced she would have a good time spending a week of her summer break in a creepy old house with her great-grandmother, her twin sister, and younger brother.

"Once you get done packing, take your suitcase and set it by the front door," her mother chuckled at seeing the frustrated look on Melissa's face.

"Fine, but I'm not going to enjoy myself." Melissa locked the clasp on the suitcase and carried it toward the door. She had just stepped out into the hallway when her little brother ran past her holding his basketball above his head.

"What the heck?" Melissa groaned.

"Move, I need to finish packing," Aaron yelled as he went into his bedroom.

"Mom, Aaron seems to think he needs to take his basketball with him in his suitcase," Melissa announced as she walked down the hallway to the living room.

"Oh, my goodness; Aaron, I told you to pack your clothes, not fill your suitcase with things you won't need."

"But I need to stay sharp on my moves if I want to make the team," Aaron groaned.

Cassy ran out of her room with a look of utter despair on her face. "Mom, I can't find my swimsuit."

"It's in the bottom drawer of your dresser."

"No, it's not. I looked there already," Cassy stood in place with her hands on her hips.

"Melissa, help your sister while I take care of Aaron."

"Mom, why can't she do it herself?" Melissa protested.

"Because Mom told you to help me, that's why." Cassy grinned then laughed when she saw the look of anger appear on her sister's face.

"Fine, I'll help her, but once we get to great-grandmother's house, she's on her own." Melissa stomped her foot then followed Cassy into her bedroom. While she loved her twin sister, she could not understand why she was so strange. She had no love of fashion or her appearance. All Cassy cared about was playing soccer and hanging out with her circle of weird friends. Melissa never understood what Cassy saw in sports and hanging with people who did not care what clothes they wore.

"I hope you're packing something other than tee-shirts and worn-out jeans," Melissa groaned as she walked into Cassy's room.

It took nearly half an hour, but all three suitcases finally sat by the front door, packed and ready to go.

"Okay, let's eat our dinner, then I want you to take your baths and get ready for bed. Your father will be home in a bit, and I'm sure he'll want to relax some before tomorrow."

After grabbing a slice of pizza, Cassy looked at her mother, "Why aren't you and Dad taking us to great-grandmother's house?"

"I've already told you. We have to be at the port to board the ship for our cruise. Your great-grandmother is sending Mr. Saunders to get you. He's a very nice man, and I promise you'll have a good time. She's a wonderful and loving woman. I'm sure you'll come to love her as much as I do."

"Mom, I don't understand how we're going to get to great-grandmother's house. Maine is a long way from here, and you haven't mentioned how we'll get there," Melissa then took a bite of pizza.

Their mother knew this next bit of news would please them, "That's where the adventure comes in. You will get to go on your great-grandmother's private jet."

"What? You mean she has her own airplane?" Aaron said, excitedly. "Wow, that's cool."

Cassy reached for another slice of pizza before speaking, "Dang, I knew she was rich, but you never said she was that rich."

"It's because it's not polite to speak in such a manner. Your great-grandmother has lived a good life, and she wanted you all to come and spend some time with her before…" she could not bring herself to finish the statement.

"She's getting old. That's what you mean, isn't it?" Melissa said, flatly.

Their mother looked at all three children and only nodded.

Cassy could see the sadness on her mother's face. "We'll have a good time visiting great-grandmother, and we promise to be good, too."

"Thank you, Cassy. I'm sure you will." She was thankful they would have this opportunity to get to know their great-grandmother.

"Hello, I'm home. Where is everyone?" a voice called out from the living room.

"We're in the kitchen eating some pizza, Steve. If you hurry, you might get some."

"Good evening, family," Steve walked into the kitchen and took his place at the table.

"Dad, Mom just told us we get to go on Great-Grandmother's private airplane. Isn't that cool?" A broad smile lit up Aaron's face.

"It sure is, and I know you will all have fun visiting her." Steve reached for a slice of pizza then set it on his plate.

"Donna, I didn't think I'd ever get things straightened out at work today. You'd think I was going to be gone for a year, not a week," he laughed then took a bite of pizza.

"I'm just glad they won't be able to call you all the time while we're on the cruise," Donna grinned.

"No, kidding. As a matter of fact, I think I'll leave my cell phone in the glove box of the car," he winked.

"That's an excellent idea." Donna knew his boss would call endlessly if he were able to reach him.

Steve glanced around the table at the faces of his beloved children. While he was excited to spend some time alone with Donna, he knew he would miss them and the crazy drama they brought to each and every day. Having two sixteen-year-old daughters and a thirteen-year-old son could make for an exciting life.

"So, is everyone packed and ready for tomorrow?" Steve saw the mixture of emotions on their faces and wondered how this visit would go for all of them.

"Yes, and I made sure not to bring any clothes that match Cassy's, too," Melissa announced as she glared across the table at Cassy.

"Good; just because we're twins doesn't mean I want to dress like you," Cassy smirked.

"Why would I want to be anything like you?" Melissa said, sarcastically.

Cassy was about to respond when their mother interrupted them. "Girls, stop it right now. I don't understand why you feel the need to argue all the time. You both used to be so close when you were younger."

Each girl glared across the table, neither willing to surrender the challenge.

Melissa and Cassy had come into the world on a cold and stormy night. Donna had felt odd the entire day, but with the due date still two weeks away, she figured she was just experiencing the usual feelings of a first-time pregnancy. Steve was working late at the office, and Donna was relaxing in bed, reading a book when her water broke. Her first impulse was to call Steve, but once the first contraction hit her, she decided it was best to call her neighbor to drive her to the hospital.

After several hours of labor, Melissa and Cassy came screaming and kicking into the world, and they had been fighting ever since.

Steve looked at his two beautiful daughters and felt his heart overflow with love. "You two will have a day when you'll need each other. I know how much you each want to be your own person, but you also need to cherish the strength you both share."

Cassy looked at Melissa and rolled her eyes. "I'd like her more if she wasn't such a Diva. She never likes to have fun. All she wants to do is shop and paint her stupid nails."

Melissa looked at Cassy with a look of utter disgust on her face. "I'd rather be a Diva than a social zero like you." Melissa stuck out her tongue, and then laughed at the angry glare on Cassy's face.

"Girls, stop it right now! You both are old enough to stop acting like two spoiled brats. I want you to promise me you'll behave yourselves while at your great-grandmother's house. The last thing she needs is to put up with a couple of arguing teenagers." Donna hated to see the girls fight, but she knew one day they would come to appreciate each other.

Of course, this brought both girls to full attention, as they realized they had pushed the subject too far.

"I'm being good, Mom," Aaron added to the conversation with an angelic expression on his face.

Donna glanced over at her sweet son and had to admit, at least he was not misbehaving. "Yes, you are. See girls, you need to learn how to behave like your brother."

Both girls turned and glared at their brother.

Aaron glared back at them with a mischievous grin on his face. Of course, this caused each girl to stick out her tongue at him.

"Mom, they stuck their tongue out at me," Aaron cried out as he tried to hide his joy at upsetting them.

"Girls, I want you two to stop this now! Okay, everyone is finished eating, so take your baths and go to bed. Tomorrow is going to be a long day." Donna struggled to hide her amusement at the way the children loved to torment each other.

The three children got up from the table without saying a word, but as they walked down the hall toward their bedrooms, Steve and Donna could hear them arguing.

"It's your fault!"

"No, it's yours!"

"I get to take my bath first."

"No, I get to go first this time."

Steve and Donna looked at each other, and it was at that moment they realized how much they would miss the children in spite of all the fighting.

Chapter 2

Everyone was up and rushing around the house trying to get ready to leave. Both girls had finished dressing and were waiting in the living room while Aaron sat at the kitchen table, still eating his breakfast.

"Aaron, you need to hurry. Mr. Saunders will be here in an hour, so get up and go get dressed," Donna groaned. She then closed her last suitcase and set it by the front door for Steve to take out to the car.

"My, you two look lovely this morning." Donna felt her heart fill with pride as she turned to look at the girls.

It had amazed Donna how much the girls looked like their great-grandmother did at their age with their long brown hair and dark, chocolate brown eyes. Donna also had to admit that even though the girls looked alike, they had entirely different personalities.

Melissa, the oldest of the twins, had always acted prim and proper. She always made sure she brushed her hair and put it up into a ponytail. She also made sure her clothes matched and were in style. Cassy, on the other hand, did not seem to care about her appearance. She was happiest in an old pair of blue jeans and an over-sized tee shirt. As for her hair, she kept it in braids, so she did not have to brush it all the time. Even though the girls were identical twins, they could not have been more different.

***

"Mom, he's here," Aaron announced as he ran into the living room.

"Aaron, go to the bathroom and comb your hair. It's a mess," Donna said sternly, as she walked to the front door.

"Oh, Mom…" Aaron groaned.

"Stop arguing; now go comb your hair."

Donna opened the front door just as Mr. Saunders was about to ring the doorbell.

"Good morning, Mrs. Moore; are the children ready?" Mr. Saunders was an attractive man in his mid-sixties with bright green eyes and graying temples. Donna had always liked him, so she was pleased he had come to get the children.

"Good morning, Mr. Saunders, it's good to see you again. The girls are ready, but Aaron still needs to comb his hair." She glanced over her shoulder toward the hallway.

"Excellent, Ma'am, I'll take the luggage out to the limousine." Mr. Saunders reached for the suitcases sitting by the front door.

"That's not necessary. Steve can do that," but no sooner had the protest left her lips than she realized her words were in vain.

"That won't be necessary. I will take care of this," he said dismissively.

Donna watched him carry the three suitcases out to the trunk of the limousine and put them inside. Once he had finished, he came back to the house and waited by the front door.

"Okay, I guess that's the best your hair is going to look today," Donna groaned, when Aaron joined them. She reached to smooth the hairs sticking up on the back of his head when Aaron pulled away.

"Sheez, Mom, it's fine."

Realizing he was no longer a little boy; she pulled her hand away. "I'm sorry, you're right; you're a young man now, aren't you?"

Donna looked at her three children and realized how much she would miss them.

"Steve, the children, are leaving," Donna shouted down the hallway to the bedrooms.

"Okay, don't let them leave until I get my goodbye kisses." Steve walked into the living room, carrying the last of the luggage.

Aaron ran up to his father and wrapped his arms around his neck. "I love you, Dad. I'm really going to miss you."

"I love you too, Aaron. I want you to promise me you'll behave yourself and just have fun." Steve held Aaron in a tight hug, not wanting to let him go.

"I will, Dad."

After a few moments, Aaron struggled to pull away. "Dad, you're crushing me."

"Oh, I'm sorry," he chuckled as he released Aaron.

Steve looked at his son and realized how he was growing up so quickly. It is hard to imagine they were now young adults, and their time of needing their parents for everything would soon end.

"Come on, they need to get going," Donna said, wiping a tear in the corner of her eye.

As they walked outside, all three children had their eyes light up with surprise.

"Wow, we get to ride in a limousine, cool!" Aaron ran toward the long, black car parked in front of their house.

"I wish Jennifer was here to see this," Melissa giggled as she ran to the car.

"I get to ride shotgun," Cassy pronounced as she ran to the passenger door.

Mr. Saunders placed his hand on the door handle preventing Cassy from opening the front passenger door. "Miss Cassandra, you will sit in the back with your sister and brother."

Cassy stopped and looked up at Mr. Saunders. She wanted to protest but thought better of it after seeing the stern look on his face.

"Yes, Sir." Without saying another word, she climbed in the back with Aaron and Melissa.

Once the children were in their places, Mr. Saunders turned to Steve and Donna. "I'm sure the children will be no trouble."

Steve briefly looked in the backseat and wondered how Donna's grandmother would ever be able to handle two sixteen-year-old girls and one rambunctious thirteen-year-old boy.

"I hope so," Steve grinned nervously.

Mr. Saunders noticed the worried expression on Steve's face. "You have nothing to fear. You two go have a lovely vacation, and I will return the children to you next week."

Steve looked at Donna and noticed the look of relief on her face. "Thank you, Mr. Saunders."

Before Mr. Saunders got into the backseat of the limousine with the children, Steve and Donna leaned down and looked inside. "Goodbye, and have a good time," they said in unison.

"Goodbye," the children all said.

Once Mr. Saunders got in the back, the driver closed the door then returned to the driver's seat.

As Steve and Donna stood on the sidewalk, watching the long, black limousine pull out on the street and drive away, they wondered what adventures lay ahead for them.

Donna turned to Steve, "Well, we need to get to the port. We don't want to miss the ship."

Chapter 3

The flight on the private jet was quite exciting for Melissa, Cassy, and Aaron. They had flown on an airplane once before, but it was not as lush as this one.

Aaron was thrilled when Mr. Saunders had shown him the laptop computer with several games he could play during the flight. Melissa had spent most of the flight talking to her friends on the private telephone while Cassy spent her time in the cockpit having the pilot explain the purpose of each button and switch on the console.

"Children, it's time to take your seats and secure your seatbelts. We will be landing soon." Mr. Saunders walked over to Aaron and took the laptop computer away from him and returned it to the secure drawer for safekeeping.

"Ah, man, I was almost done with that level," Aaron whined.

"I'm sure you will have the opportunity to complete that level on the flight home." Mr. Saunders locked the drawer holding the computer.

"Wow, is that great-grandmother's house?" Melissa said excitedly as she pointed out of the window at the vast mansion overlooking the Atlantic Ocean.

"Yes, it is. Now, please sit, Miss Melissa," Mr. Saunders said in a stern tone.

"Dang, it's big like a castle," Cassy grinned. Cassy was amazed at the stone mansion with what appeared to be a tall tower facing out over the ocean. She had faint memories of visiting her great-grandmother in the big castle years ago, but she had come to believe it was nothing more than the false memories of a small child.

"This is really cool. She does live in a castle," Cassy giggled softly.

"Yes, it is, Miss Cassandra. Now, please sit." Mr. Saunders checked each child's seatbelt before taking his own seat.

***

The Wilham estate overlooked the Atlantic Ocean, on one of the many small islands dotting the Maine coastline. The family had settled on the island nearly two-hundred years ago when the first of the Wilham's decided to come to America.

James Wilham had started the family business with one small fishing boat, but over the years, his business grew into one of the largest fleets in the area. He had built the sprawling mansion on the east side of the island so his wife could always watch for him to return from his time at sea.

The joys and pains of life had filled the house over the years, from the births of children to the death of loved ones. Abigail Wilham was born on a cold winter's night in the old house. She had come into the world, crying and ready to face whatever adventures life had for her. Her parents had loved her dearly and had plans for their lives, but on a warm summer's eve, they both died in an automobile accident on their way home from an outing in the city.

Of course, this had devastated Abigail, as her parents were her world, but with time and the love of her grandfather, she had learned to laugh again.

Thomas Wilham traveled the world because of his business, so each time he would return home, it was a grand affair. The house servants would always prepare a special meal with all the grandeur a little girl would desire. The table was set with the most elegant bone china and crystal, the soft glow of candles filled the room, and Abigail would dress in a beautiful gown while her Grandfather donned his best tuxedo with tails.

On one of his trips, Abigail's grandfather had returned with a special gift for her. It was an old book bound in leather and a large, red jewel placed in the center of the outer cover.

"Oh, Grandfather, it's beautiful." Abigail reached for the book, wanting to look more closely at it.

"My dear, this is not a book you read as the others in our library. It's ancient and extremely valuable. Do you see the red stone?"

Abigail nodded her head with her eyes transfixed on the jewel.

"I was told it's called The Blood Key. It's a perfectly cut ruby stone, so you must be careful with it. I have a man making a glass case to keep the book in for safekeeping, but will allow us to still see it." Her grandfather was saddened when he saw the disappointed look on her face.

"But Grandfather, can't I read it just once? I promise not to damage it," Abigail pleaded.

Her grandfather reached out and gently touched her cheek. "I'm sorry, my dear, but I need you to promise me you will not touch the book. It's very fragile, so touching the pages may cause damage that cannot be repaired."

Abigail looked down at the deep, red stone and could not help but wonder why it seemed to draw her to it. She wanted to protest again, but she knew her grandfather would not change his mind.

"Yes, Grandfather, I promise," she said with tears of sadness in her eyes.

***

As the weeks passed by, Abigail would sneak into the library to stare at the strange book for hours at a time. She wanted to open the glass case, but she had promised her grandfather she would leave it alone. For some odd reason, just having the book nearby seemed to ease her loneliness whenever her grandfather was away on his business trips.

Yet, sometimes life gives us an unexpected twist. One afternoon, the tragic news arrived that her grandfather's airplane was missing. He was on his way home but had flown into a storm, and no one had heard from him since. Abigail had paced the halls of the old house, waiting for news of her grandfather's return, but with each passing day, his chance for a safe return grew slim.

Everyone had tried to convince her he was gone, but in her heart, she knew he would return to her as he had always promised. Her grandfather was the center of her world, so Abigail was not prepared to accept his death.

She had tried to be brave, but as the days progressed, she felt more alone. One afternoon, while wandering around the large house, she ended up in the library, gazing at the mysterious book in the glass case. She had glanced around the room as though her grandfather would walk through the door at any instant and remind her to leave the book alone, but it was not to happen.

"Grandfather, why did you leave me? I live in this house full of servants, yet I still feel alone. Please come back to me," Abigail cried as she rested her hand on top of the glass case.

Through her tears, she suddenly felt a strange sensation move through her hand. It was a soft tingling, like the wings of butterflies fluttering against her skin.

Abigail quickly pulled her hand away and noticed how the tingling had stopped. She examined her hand, and when finding nothing, she placed it on the glass box again.

"How strange, I don't remember it doing that before," Abigail giggled softly to herself.

"I wonder..." Abigail held her breath and slowly opened the glass case.

Suddenly, without warning, bright-colored lights shot from the glass box like fireworks filling the night sky. The vibrant lights filled the room, dancing in the air. Abigail jumped back, unsure of what was happening until she heard a soft voice come from inside the box.

"Come to me, Abigail."

"What? Who are you?" Abigail stepped forward and looked down at the book.

"Come to me, Abigail," the voice repeated. Abigail now noticed the ruby stone attached to the book began to glow and pulsate like a beating heart.

"Please, Abigail, we need your help," the voice pleaded.

Abigail did not know what to do. Was this actually happening, or was it some sort of dream? More of the brightly colored lights shot from the box, but this time, they wrapped around Abigail, spinning so quickly she began to feel dizzy.

"Please help us, Abigail. All you need to do is touch the Blood Key," the voice cried out with urgency.

Abigail's mind spun wildly as she reached out and touched the red stone, and in a flash of light, she was gone.

Chapter 4

Melissa, Cassy, and Aaron stood looking up at the massive mansion with its stone steps leading up to the large wrap-around porch.

"Wow, great-grandmother has a huge house," Melissa said.

"Yeah, it's nice, but check out the ocean. It goes on forever." Cassy pointed out over the water.

"This is going to be so cool." Aaron's eyes glistened with excitement as he looked around the grounds.

"Come, children, your great-grandmother is waiting for you." Mr. Saunders motioned for them to follow him as he walked up the stone steps toward the large entry door.

The children all exchanged glances. They then turned and followed Mr. Saunders, each wondering what their time here would bring.

Once inside, they were amazed at how the inside of the house looked like the museum they went to on their school field trip. There were paintings on the walls, and other elegant and old looking objects sitting around the large entryway.

"Follow me." Mr. Saunders walked toward a large wooden door on the right side of the entryway. He reached for the oversized brass doorknob and then opened the door.

"She's waiting for you inside." Mr. Saunders stepped aside, allowing the children to pass.

Once they had entered the large room, each of them wondered what was about to happen. The beautifully decorated room took Cassy's breath away. There was a tall grandfather's clock sitting in the corner and the painting of a man above the massive stone fireplace. Cassy assumed the man in the painting was someone of importance.

Next, the children saw a white sofa with carved wooden legs and two matching chairs. Cassy was surprised to see an elegant older woman sitting in one of the chairs.

"Come closer so I may see you better," the woman said in a gentle tone.

After exchanging nervous glances, Cassy, Melissa, and Aaron slowly walked toward the woman. Once they stood in front of her, she smiled, which helped to ease their nerves.

"Please, sit on the sofa, so we may get to know each other better. It's been so long since I've seen you, and you've all grown so much."

Once they had taken their place on the sofa, Cassy, Melissa, and Aaron quietly waited.

"Are you thirsty?"

"Yes, and I'm hungry, too," Aaron spoke up with enthusiasm.

"Oh, my, we need to get you something to eat then. Are you ladies hungry as well?"

Both girls nodded their heads.

"Great-grandmother?" Cassy began to ask the question stirring in her mind then suddenly changed her mind.

"Yes, my dear, but you don't need to refer to me as Great-Grandmother, you may call me by my name if you wish." She then smiled when she saw the surprised expressions appear on their faces. "You may call me Abigail. Here, let me have the kitchen staff make us all a snack."

Abigail reached down and pushed the button on a small box sitting on the table next to her chair. She then told the cook to prepare a snack fit for two lovely princesses and a handsome prince.

"If we are princesses and a prince, then that makes you our Queen. I think we should call you, Queen Abigail." Melissa loved the idea of being royalty, and she had to admit Abigail had the elegance of a Queen in the way she spoke and her mannerisms. Yes, the title of Queen Abigail suited her perfectly.

Cassy and Aaron agreed, and from that moment on, they all knew this visit was going to be special.

***

Once they had all finished their snack, the children asked for a tour of the house. Abigail was thrilled to have them there, as the house had seemed so empty the last few years after the death of her husband. They had lived many happy years on the vast estate, but after several months of failing health, he had died and left Abigail alone.

Their son, who was Donna's father, had traveled the world for the family business. Unfortunately, on one of the trips when he had taken her mother along, they both had died in a tragic boating accident. This had brought Donna to live on the island, until the day she went off to college, never to return except for an occasional visit.

***

"Why is your house so big, Queen Abigail? You could fit our entire house in your living room and dining room," Melissa teased.

"Yeah, this is bigger than the fancy hotel we stayed in when we went on vacation last time," Cassy agreed as she admired the large room.

Abigail looked into the faces of her beloved great-grandchildren and realized they were correct. "You know something, it is rather large. I've lived here so long I no longer notice."

"How long have you lived here?" Aaron asked.

"Let me think for a moment. I would say I have lived here for over seventy years. Oh my, the years have flown by so quickly." Abigail laughed to herself at realizing how long she had lived in this house.

"Wow, seventy years; you must be really old," Aaron shook his head, trying to understand how old she must be.

"Aaron, that's not nice to say," Melissa scolded him.

"That's quite alright. As a matter of fact, my handsome Prince, I am old. I turned eight-four-years-old just last month." Abigail saw the shocked look on Aaron's face and could not help but feel the love in her heart grow for this wonderful young man. "On the other hand, I must admit having you here makes me feel much younger."

"And we're glad to be here with you, Queen Abigail," Melissa said as she stepped forward and gave Abigail a hug.

"You are such a sweet little Princess, Melissa," Abigail smiled as she returned the hug.

Seeing the joy on their great-grandmother's face, Cassy, and Aaron both stepped forward and joined in on the hugs.

"Oh my, I am such a lucky Queen to have my special little Prince and Princesses here with me."

Once they had finished sharing their hugs, they decided to continue the tour of the house.

"What's in this room?" Cassy pointed toward the large oak door with the shiny brass doorknob at the end of the long hallway.

"This is my favorite room in the whole house." Abigail's eyes lit up with joy as she walked to the door and opened it. She then stepped aside, allowing the children to enter.

"Wow, you have your own library," Cassy cried out.

"Look at all these books," Melissa's eyes lit up with surprise as she walked over to the long shelf, filled with books.

Aaron, though, was not as impressed. He stood in place and looked around the room with the expression on his face of someone who wanted to be anywhere else but there.

"What's wrong, my Prince? Don't you like books?" Abigail rested her hand on his shoulder, bringing him out of his daze.

"No, not really," Aaron whispered, not wanting to upset her.

"Maybe we can find one in here you would enjoy. Let's see, do you like pirates?" Abigail laughed when she saw the excited look appear on Aaron's face.

"I know just the book for you, my Prince." She offered him her hand. "Come with me."

Aaron took Abigail by the hand. "Will it have sword fights and buried treasure?"

"Oh, yes, and much more." Abigail had read this book many times over the years and had enjoyed it greatly.

"Queen Abigail, what's this book?" Cassy asked as she looked at the mysterious-looking book locked inside a glass case.

Abigail walked toward the table in the center of the library with the glass case holding the book given to her all those years ago.

"My grandfather brought that book to me from a far-off land when I was about your age. It's old and very fragile, so it must stay in the glass case for its protection."

"But, can't we read it?" Melissa did not understand why the book was locked in the glass case.

"No, it must never be taken from that case. There are hundreds of other books for you to enjoy, but I'm sorry, that book is not one of them." Abigail could see the disappointment in the girl's eyes, but she held firm. "Now, let's continue our tour of the house."

They all turned and walked toward the large oak door, and as Abigail held the door open, Cassy glanced back at the strange book locked inside of the glass case.

What mysteries do you hold? Cassy thought to herself as the image of the book burned into her mind.

The remainder of the afternoon, they had spent exploring the rest of the house and the grounds. Once they returned to the house, the children went to their rooms and found the maid had put their belongings away and laid out their clothes for dinner.

"I could get used to this." Melissa pointed to the other door in her room. "Look, we have a bathroom between our rooms."

"I know, isn't that cool? Hey, I wonder if Mom and Dad would get us a maid," Cassy said playfully.

"Children, you need to get cleaned up and change into the clean clothes I laid out for you. Dinner will be served in a half an hour," Pricilla, the upstairs maid, announced as she glanced inside Melissa's room.

Melissa was about to ask why they needed to change clothes when Aaron came running into her room.

"I have the coolest room. It has pictures of ships and one of those old-time periscopes that pirates used on their ships. I looked through it, and I could see way out over the ocean."

Pricilla looked at Aaron and could not help but laugh. "I'm glad you approve of your room, but you need to go get ready for dinner. I have left a washcloth and towel in your bathroom and clean clothes on your bed. Now hurry, because we don't want your great-grandmother to wait for you."

Pricilla turned and looked at Melissa and Cassy. "Please get yourselves ready and then go downstairs. The cook has prepared a grand feast."

Chapter 5

When Cassy, Melissa, and Aaron entered the dining room, they were surprised to see the formal setting. Delicate bone china dishware sat on a crisply ironed tablecloth with crystal goblets and silver flatware, all awaiting the grand feast.

Abigail sat at the head of the long table, with one place setting to her right and two place settings to her left.

"Please join me." Abigail motioned for them to take their places at the table.

Each took their seats, unsure of how to act.

Cassy was the first to speak. "Queen Abigail, why is everything so fancy?"

Melissa and Aaron exchanged glances and then nodded their heads in agreement.

"I was taught when one has distinguished guests, the evening meal is always to be a grand affair. It has been far too long since I've had guests, so I wanted to make this a special time for us all."

As the children looked at the fancy table setting, they worried about what sort of meal was planned for them. Anytime their mother had set the table like this, the food was not anything they would consider a feast.

"First, we put our napkins on our laps." Abigail lifted her napkin and spread it out on her lap then she waited as the children did the same.

"Wonderful. Please bring the feast," Abigail said to the servers standing along the back wall of the dining room.

To the delight of each child, the servers brought slices of cheese pizza and placed it on their plates. Then they filled the crystal goblets with strawberry soda.

"Queen Abigail, you are so cool," Aaron said as he shoved a slice of pizza in his mouth.

"How did you know we love cheese pizza and strawberry soda?" Melissa said, excitedly.

"A Queen always knows what her Prince and Princesses want," Abigail winked.

"I think this is the best pizza I've ever had," Cassy grinned as she picked up the goblet and took a drink.

"I'm glad you are pleased. Servers, bring my young Prince and Princesses some more pizza."

***

After they had finished eating their meal and ice cream for dessert, they all went to the library.

"You really don't have any television here?" Aaron looked around the room.

"No, I've never enjoyed watching it. I find reading a good book in the evening is quite relaxing." Abigail saw the disappointed looks on their faces, but she hoped they would find a book to their liking.

"Well, can you show me that book about pirates?" Aaron asked.

"Of course, follow me. You ladies can look around and see if you can find a book to your liking as well." Abigail took Aaron by the hand and walked over to the shelves by the window. "Let's see, where is that book about pirates?"

Melissa and Cassy walked toward the shelves by the large fireplace but stopped at the table with the book inside of the glass case.

"I wonder why we can't read this one," Cassy whispered.

"It's because it's old and she doesn't want it ruined, that's why." Melissa tugged on Cassy's arm, pulling her toward the shelves with the other books.

Cassy reached out with her other hand and was about to touch the top of the glass box when...

"Stop it; you don't want to upset her, do you?" Melissa scolded her sister.

"Okay, I'll leave it alone," Cassy pulled her hand away and followed Melissa.

"Look, I have a book about pirates. Queen Abigail said it has sword fights, hidden treasure, and all sorts of fun things in it. I'm going to start reading it now." Aaron rushed over to one of the over-stuffed chairs and settled in with the book on his lap.

Abigail walked up to the girls and could see the blank expressions on their faces as they looked at the rows of books on the shelves in front of them.

"What sort of stories do you enjoy? I bet I know what books you like, Princess Melissa. I bet you'd like a story about a Prince and Princess who find each other and fall in love. Am I correct?"

Melissa looked up at Abigail and blushed.

"I knew it." Abigail reached up above her head and pulled down an old, worn book.

"Here was one of my favorites when I was your age. I'm sure you will love it as much as I did." She handed the book to Melissa, who thanked her before walking over to another over-stuffed chair.

Abigail then looked at Cassy. "Let's see, you seem to be an adventurous spirit, so I bet you would enjoy a book about dragons. Am I correct?"

Cassy looked at Abigail with a surprising glint in her eyes and nodded, letting her great-grandmother know she had chosen well.

"Let's see, I think this one will be just what you need." Abigail reached for a large book with a picture of a fire-breathing dragon on the cover. "This is a fascinating tale. I have read this one several times."

Cassy took the book and ran over to the chair next to Melissa and sat with the large book on her lap. "Thank you, Queen Abigail."

"Yes, thank you," Melissa and Aaron chimed in.

"You are all very welcome." Abigail walked over to the last chair and took the book off the table next to it, and then she glanced at the children who were now lost in their own world of imagination. Opening her own book, she began to read.

**

No one realized how late it was until the grandfather clock in the corner chimed ten times.

"Oh my, it's late. Why don't we put our books down for now and go upstairs to bed? We have a busy day tomorrow," Abigail announced as she stood and stretched.

"I'm not sleepy, I want to keep reading," Aaron complained as he held tightly to his book.

"My dear, I'm thrilled you are enjoying the tale of pirates and buried treasure, but it is time for bed. I promise you'll get to continue on your adventure tomorrow." Abigail reached down and took his book. Putting the string page marker in place, she then set the book on the table next to his chair.

Seeing there was no sense in arguing, Melissa and Cassy closed their books and set them on the table next to Aaron's book.

"Queen Abigail, thank you for the wonderful day. I'm so happy we came to visit you," Melissa said, as Cassy and Aaron nodded their agreement.

A deep love surged through Abigail's heart. "I'm happy you came as well. Now, up to your rooms and go to bed. Tomorrow I have an exciting day planned for us."

Each of the children took turns, giving Abigail a hug and kiss before going upstairs to their rooms. As Abigail watched them leave the room, she said a silent prayer of thanks for this time with her little Prince and Princesses.

***

Darkness, along with an eerie quiet, filled the room. Cassy had tossed and turned for what seemed like an eternity, but still was unable to fall asleep. She decided to get up and go back down to the library and read some more of her book with the hope she would finally be able to fall asleep.

Slowly opening her bedroom door, Cassy stepped out into the hallway. She looked in both directions to make sure no one was awake. Cassy then tip-toed toward the stairs, hoping the old wooden floor would not alert someone of her presence. Once she was downstairs, she headed straight to the library.

Cassy opened the door to the library and slipped inside, but what she saw froze her in her tracks.

"What are you doing up?" Cassy whispered.

"What are you doing?" Aaron whispered as he tried to see if she was alone.

"I couldn't sleep, so I came down here to read some more of my book," Cassy said defensively.

"Well, I couldn't sleep until I found out what happened to the pirate captain," Aaron groaned.

"Fine; I won't tell if you don't, okay?" Cassy looked at Aaron, hoping he would agree.

"It's a deal," he held out his hand.

"Good," Cassy took his hand in hers, and they sealed the promise with a handshake. She then walked over to the chair, where she had sat earlier and picked up her book.

Cassy looked at Aaron and grinned, "Mom and Dad would never believe we snuck out of bed to read a book."

Aaron nodded his agreement, then he returned his attention to his exciting tale of pirates and buried treasure.

***

Silence filled the room while Cassy read her story of fire-breathing dragons and great battles when she suddenly heard a strange sound.

She glanced over at Aaron and saw he was lost in his world of pirates, so she returned to her reading.

"Please, help us," the soft voice seemed to float on the air.

"Did you hear that?" Cassy asked Aaron.

"Hear what? I didn't hear anything. Leave me alone, it's getting exciting now," Aaron groaned as he pulled the book up close to his face.

"Please, we need your help," the voice repeated, but slightly louder this time.

"Come on, didn't you hear it?" Cassy set her book on the table and stood, looking around the room.

"You must be hearing things," Aaron rolled his eyes at how silly she was acting.

"Please, help us," the voice cried out with urgency.

Cassy glanced over at Aaron and saw the surprised look on his face.

"You heard it, didn't you?"

"Yeah, what do you think it is?" Aaron looked around the room nervously.

"I don't know, but it's coming from over there." Cassy pointed toward the center of the room where the table with the book in the glass case sat.

Cassy and Aaron exchanged glances then slowly began to walk toward the table.

"Please, help us. Save us from the Evil Queen," the voice cried out.

Cassy's gaze met Aaron's, each wondering if this was a dream.

"Yeah, I heard it too." Aaron suddenly felt a sense of dread churning up from deep inside of him.

They both stepped up to the table and looked down at the book.

"How is this possible?" Cassy's eyes were transfixed on the book.

"I don't know, but that book is talking to us." Aaron shook his head, hoping they would awaken from this strange dream.

Cassy held her breath before gently placing her hand on the top of the glass box. No sooner had her hand touched the glass than the lock on the box opened and fell to the floor.

"You broke it," Aaron cried out.

"No, I didn't, it did that itself." Cassy quickly pulled her hand away.

Aaron read Cassy's mind, and he knew what she was thinking. "Don't do it. You heard what great-grandmother said. We're supposed to leave this book alone."

"I won't hurt it. I only want to see it better." Cassy reached for the handle on the lid and slowly lifted it.

Suddenly, without warning, the lid flew out of Cassy's hand and bright-colored lights of red, green, and blue shot out of the box and filled the room.

Cassy found herself trapped in the lights as they wrapped around her in a swirling whirlwind of glowing fog. She tried to step away but found she was unable to move her feet.

Aaron stood transfixed, watching the lights dance around the room. Suddenly, they moved toward Cassy, surrounding her in a whirlwind of flashing colors. Fear gripped Aaron. However, before he could react, he found himself caught up in the same whirlwind of lights.

"Cassy, what's happening?" Aaron cried out.

"I don't know." She looked down at the book and noticed the Ruby glowing with more of the bright colors shooting from its center.

Aaron watched in horror as the lights wrapped around Cassy and lifted her up into the air above the book.

An overwhelming fear gripped Cassy. As the lights held her hostage, she found she was unable to scream or free herself from their force.

Cassy looked at Aaron for help, but when their gazes met, Aaron suddenly found himself trapped by the same lights as they lifted him into the air. He struggled to shout for help but found himself unable to speak.

Panic filled their hearts as the room spun around them, causing them to grow dizzy and disoriented. They were about to give up all hope of escape when a bright flash of light filled the room, and once it was gone, it had taken Cassy and Aaron with it.

Chapter 6

Cassy felt horrible. She was dizzy and had a throbbing pain in her head.

"Dang, I don't feel so good," she moaned.

"Cassy, where are we?" Aaron spoke in a near whisper.

"Huh? What are you talking about, we're in the library," Cassy groaned as she opened her eyes. Nevertheless, what she saw made it entirely clear they were no longer in the library. "Aaron, where did you get those clothes?"

"I was about to ask you the same question. These sure don't look like our pajamas."

Before Cassy could respond, she heard the crunching of leaves. "Who's there?"

"Abigail, you have returned to us," a voice exclaimed from behind a fallen tree.

Cassy struggled to her feet then helped Aaron to stand.

"Cassy, who said that?"

"I don't know."

"Who are you? Come out so we can see you." Cassy pushed Aaron behind her in a protective stance.

"You are not Abigail? I do not understand You look like Abigail from the stories I grew up hearing," the voice was full of disappointment at hearing this news.

Cassy squared her shoulders, trying to summon the courage to face this unknown person.

"Show yourself," she demanded.

Aaron gasped as he watched a creature step from behind the log. It stood nearly five-foot-tall with dark scaly skin and bright emerald green eyes that seemed to look deep into his soul. He blinked his eyes several times, not convinced he was indeed seeing what was stood there before him.

"You're a dragon," the words escaped his mouth before he realized what he had said.

The creature stepped closer but stopped when Cassy held out her hand. "Stop, dragons aren't real. They are only make-believe, something out of Fairy Tales."

The expression on the creature's face changed from one of hope to one of sadness.

"I do not understand. There are whispers of how Abigail, the chosen Champion, who had fought the Evil Queen Alona, would someday return. It is said once she returns, she will defeat the Queen and restore freedom to the Kingdom of Walandra. You promised that you would return to help us, and here you are."

Cassy shook her head, trying to clear her mind. "Stop calling me Abigail. My name is Cassy. I don't know you, and I never promised to return. Heck, I don't even know where we are, so how could I have promised anything?"

"But you answered our plea. We called out to you, and you returned to Walandra," the creature smiled, trying to put her at ease. "You must remember."

Cassy shook her head again, then she looked back at Aaron. "Pinch me. I want to wake up from this strange dream."

Aaron looked at Cassy and chuckled. "Pinch you, I've already been pinching myself, and it's not working. I don't think we're dreaming. This is real."

The words hit Cassy with such force she nearly collapsed to the ground.

This is real, but how is that possible?

Cassy looked at the creature again when suddenly her mind filled with thoughts, not her own.

Yes, this is real. You are in the Kingdom of Walandra. I am your friend, Frair, please try to remember," the voice said in a friendly tone.

"Stop it, and get out of my head," Cassy cried out as she cupped her hands over her ears.

Frair looked at Cassy and realized she did not believe. Sadness filled his heart at knowing without her help, the curse would continue to enslave the Kingdom.

"I am sorry I was mistaken. I thought you were Abigail, returning to free us from the curse of the Evil Queen." Frair's shoulders slumped as his eyes lost their luster and filled with tears.

"Why would you think I'm this person you call Abigail?" Cassy looked at Frair with anger burning on her face.

Frair looked deeply into her eyes, searching for a hint of Abigail hidden behind the anger. "You're right; you are not the Abigail of the stories. It's just you wear the sacred Dragon's Breast Plate with the Blood Key."

Cassy was about to protest when Aaron stepped around in front of her.

"He's right, look." Aaron pointed a shaky finger at the unusual looking plate with what appeared to be the red stone from the book placed in its center.

"Look, the plate looks just like one of the scales covering his body, only much larger," Aaron cried out.

Cassy looked down at her chest. "How did that get there? This isn't possible. I never put this on."

"One does not put on the sacred Breast Plate with the Blood Key. It only chooses those who are worthy. You may not be Abigail, but you have been selected to fight the Evil Queen and release the subjects of Walandra from her curse." Frair stepped forward and bowed his head in reverence.

Cassy's mind was swirling when it suddenly came to her. "This Abigail you speak of must be our great-grandmother. We came to visit her, and the book was in her library. Are you telling us she is the Abigail who fought the Evil Queen the last time?"

Frair stood silent for several moments, trying to understand her words. "That is why the Blood Key called out to you. You share the same bloodline as Abigail. Oh, how wonderful that you will save us."

He then opened his wings to their full length in joyous celebration.

"Cool, he has wings," Aaron grinned as he pointed toward the outstretched wings. "Can you fly?"

"Yes, but not for long distances; I am still too young," Frair pulled his wings back in and tucked them behind his back.

"Too cool, may I touch you?" Aaron reached out his hand then stopped when Cassy pulled him back.

"Don't do that. We still don't know if we can trust him," Cassy growled while glaring at Frair.

At hearing her words, Frair stepped back, putting more distance between them.

"Look, you hurt his feelings," Aaron groaned as he pulled away from her. "I'm sorry my sister is such a creep."

Frair looked at the surprised expression on Cassy's face at her brother's words and laughed. "Yes, I can tell she can be a bit moody. You may touch me if you wish."

Aaron slowly stepped toward Frair then gently touched his scaly shoulder.

"Cool, I always wondered what a dragon felt like. I always thought the scales would be hard and sharp to the touch, but they feel smooth like the velvet on Mom's pillows on the couch. Check this out," Aaron grinned as he walked around behind Frair.

Cassy kept her distance, still unsure if she should trust this strange creature. Her mind kept telling her to stay away, but a small voice from deep inside of her heart told her he could be trusted. She reached out to touch him when there was a rustling in the leaves from behind them.

"Who's there?" Cassy demanded as she spun around.

"It is I, Roupert. Who are you?" he said in a firm voice as he stepped out of the thick trees.

Once his eyes met Cassy's, he dropped to one knee. "Abigail, you have returned as promised."

Cassy glanced at Frair then back to Roupert.

"How many times do I have to say I am not Abigail? She's my great-grandmother. My name is Cassy," frustration dripped from each word.

Roupert rose to his feet and looked closely at Cassy. He could see the resemblance, but there was something different in her eyes. "Yes, I realize you are not Abigail. I am sorry for the confusion."

"She may not be Abigail, but she has a strong spirit. Otherwise, the Blood Key would not have chosen her," Frair said with a spark of excitement in his voice. "Look, she wears the sacred Breast Plate with the Blood Key."

Roupert quickly looked back at Cassy and saw she, in fact, wore the Breast Plate. "So, it is as foretold. Our champion has come to release us from the rule of the Evil Queen Alona."

Cassy looked intently at Roupert, unsure if she had heard him correctly. "What do you mean by your champion has come? Are you talking about me?"

She laughed nervously at the idea of her winning a battle against an Evil Queen.

Roupert gazed into Cassy's eyes. "That is precisely what I mean. The Blood Key would not have chosen you, otherwise."

"Wow, how cool is that?" Aaron exclaimed. "I always knew you were tough, but I never thought you would do battle with an Evil Queen. Do I get to help?"

Cassy shot Aaron an angry look. "No, you don't get to help because I'm not going to battle anyone."

"But… you have to…"

Cassy interrupted before Aaron could continue. "I don't have to do anything other than try and get us back home."

Shaking their heads, Frair and Roupert showed their disappointment.

"What, what's wrong? Is there going to be a problem with us going home?" Cassy suddenly felt a sickening feeling grow in her stomach.

Roupert stepped forward and held out his hand. "It is getting late. I invite you to join me for the night in my cabin. The forest gets cold at night, and I'm sure you must be tired and hungry."

Cassy looked at Roupert, unsure if she should trust him. She then looked at Aaron and realized she had no choice.

"Okay, but only for one night. We need to figure out how to get back before they realize we're gone," Cassy reached out and took Aaron by the hand. "Lead the way."

Chapter 7

The glow of the fire filling the room made Cassy and Aaron feel safe and comfortable. They had enjoyed a tasty meal of stew and bread and were now sitting on straw-filled mats spread out on the floor.

Cassy and Aaron were surprised how comfortable Roupert had made the small one-room hut. In the center of the room, there was a firepit, which he used for cooking and heat. Along the walls in the back of the hut were shelves filled with jars and pouches, as well as two large books. On the opposite side of the hut from was a small wooden table and chairs, along with shelves for his dishes.

"Thank you for the meal and a place to sleep," Cassy said, as she pulled the blanket around her. "I have to admit I've never slept on a straw bed before."

Roupert put the last of the bowls on the shelf then he joined them by the fire. "Really, what sort of bed do you sleep on?"

Cassy thought for a moment. "I'm not sure what it's made of, but I know it's not straw." She smiled when she saw the confused expression on Roupert's face.

Aaron sat up and looked toward the window by the door with a sad expression on his face.

"Why is Frair sleeping outside? Won't he get cold out there?"

Roupert shook his head and laughed. "Frair will be just fine outside. I invited him to sleep inside once during a severe storm, but he sneezed and almost burned my hut to the ground."

"Oh, my, how horrible," Cassy gasped.

"After that, we both agreed it was best he stay outside. Though, I did build him shelter so he could stay out of the weather. It's made of sturdy wood and stone. He tells me he is quite comfortable."

Aaron yawned and rubbed his eyes. "I'm sleepy." He rolled over on his side, facing the wall with the fire to his back, and after a few moments, he was sound asleep.

After a few quiet minutes, Cassy wondered the best way to approach Roupert on the subject swirling around in her mind. He looked at her and could tell she was struggling with her thoughts.

"You look distressed, Cassy. You seem to have a question tormenting your mind."

"Yes, I do, but there's something I don't understand. Why isn't Frair with other dragons? What kind of curse did the Evil Queen cast over the kingdom?"

Roupert leaned back against a wood bucket and nervously ran his hand through his dark, wavy hair. Many years had passed since he had spoken aloud of the curse, and honestly, he had hoped he would never have to speak of it again. He cleared his throat and began.

"For thousands of years, the Kingdom of Walandra was ruled by the mighty Ashlym, the King of the Dragons and his lovely wife, Queen Privlana. King Ashlym ruled the subjects of Walandra with both kindness and respect, and the kingdom had flourished under his rule. Over the years, each subject of the kingdom enjoyed a life of happiness and freedom from fear. Everything was perfect until she came."

Roupert paused a moment, fighting the anger he felt at remembering that horrible time. "Alona had pretended to be a slave running from a cruel master, and she convinced Queen Privlana to allow her to take refuge in the castle. Alona had played her part well in her game of deception. She had treated everyone with respect and kindness, even the lowest of castle servants, which pleased King Ashlym, as he believed everyone deserved respect regardless of their station in life."

Roupert reached behind him and pulled a piece of wood from the bucket and tossed it into the fire. Once it began to burn, he continued.

"It was a dark day for the kingdom when Alona made her move. None in the kingdom knew she was, in fact, an evil Sorceress from a far-off land, as she had fooled everyone with her magic. Before coming to Walandra, she had cast a spell on herself to conceal her true self. No one saw the evil beating within her dark heart, not even King Ashlym," Roupert shook his head, feeling despair at how Alona had fooled the entire kingdom.

"Alona had come to Walandra to steal the powerful magic of the Dragon and make it her own. She knew the Queen was trusting and always willing to help those in need. For that reason, she knew if she acted the victim of a cruel master, the Queen would grant her sanctuary and would protect her." Rage burned in Roupert at how Alona had betrayed the trust the Queen had in her.

"At first, the King was unsure if they should allow Alona to stay in the castle, but the Queen had begged him to grant her mercy, so he finally relented and granted her sanctuary. Several weeks had passed without occurrence when one day, the unthinkable happened. King Ashlym had taken his human form and was resting in the Royal Chamber when…"

"Wait a minute, what do you mean by human form?" Cassy interrupted.

Roupert looked at the surprised expression on Cassy's face and smiled. "You did not know that Dragons can change into a human form?"

Cassy gaped at Roupert with a dumbfounded expression on her face, "No, I've never heard anything like that before."

"Well, they do. You see, Dragons are magical creatures and can do the most miraculous things. From the dawn of time, all Royal Families were from the lineage of the Dragon. Is it not like that in your realm?"

Cassy looked at Roupert and merely shrugged her shoulders.

"Well, in the Kingdom of Walandra, it has always been so," Roupert grinned when he saw understanding appear on Cassy's face.

"So, does that mean Frair is a member of the Royal Family?"

"That is a subject for a later time," Roupert said flatly.

"So, what happened next? What happened to King Ashlym in the Royal Chamber?" Cassy asked.

Roupert hung his head as sadness filled his heart. "The King had no idea of the depth of Alona's deceit. As he lay in the Royal Bedchamber, Alona came to him cloaked by magic in the human form of Queen Privlana. The King, at not knowing of Alona's treachery allowed her to lie on the bed next to him. You see, Alona had prepared well for her mission to kill the King. She had managed to cast a spell over the Guardian of the Dagger of Destiny, which was the only instrument created that could kill a Dragon. All that one had to do was to strike the Dragon in the heart while it was in its human form. Yet, Alona had more plans for the dead King. She had found one of the lost Blood Stones that if struck with the blood of a mighty Dragon, would bestow the bearer the magical powers of the Dragon. This was Alona's goal from the beginning. She wanted to rule Walandra by enslaving the Dragons and using their power to ensure her reign."

Cassy found herself transfixed, as Roupert told the tale of how the Evil Queen Alona took control of the Kingdom, and she wondered what her part would be in freeing them from her rule.

"So, what happened next?" Cassy said with her eyes wide with fear.

Roupert cleared his throat then continued with his story.

~~~

"As King Ashlym lay on his back asleep, Alona lifted the knife and plunged it deep into his heart. Then as she pulled it from his heart, she heard a scream come from the doorway. It was Queen Privlana, with a look of horror on her face. Realizing she must act quickly, Alona jumped up from the bed while holding the bloodied knife in her hand.

"What have you done?" Queen Privlana cried out.

"I have killed the King and taken his blood." Alona then reached into her pocket and pulled out the Blood Stone.

"With his blood, I cast a spell over the house of Dragons. You, Queen Privlana, will forever be my slave, and the remainder of your family will die. With your magical power and that of the King's blood, I will rule over the Kingdom of Walandra for all time." Alona then laughed as she raised the dagger above her head."

~~~

Cassy sat up. "No way, no way can she win. It's wrong," she whispered, so as not to awaken Aaron.

Roupert looked at Cassy, feeling amused by her excitement. "Sit, my young friend, and I will continue with the tale."

Cassy knew there was no sense in arguing with him, so she lay back down on her mat without saying another word.

"Okay, let me see where I was," Roupert rubbed his chin, then continued with his tale.

~~~

Alona held the dagger above her head and was about to strike the Blood Stone when Queen Privlana transformed into her Dragon form.

Standing nearly twenty feet tall with smoke puffing from her nostrils, she looked down at Alona and spoke in a firm voice, "I cast a spell that you are forever denied power over the Blood Stone. It and its great power will be gone from this realm until brought back by a Champion. I also cast a spell over my Dragon family, transforming them into stone, thus protecting them from death by your hand."

Privlana's tone was dark and menacing as she continued, "You may rule this kingdom, but one day a brave soul will come and through great sacrifice will return my husband's blood to me. For you see, the Blood Stone is now a key, which will reverse your curse upon this kingdom. You may possess dark powers, but they will not extend beyond the borders of this realm."

Alona looked at the Queen and laughed, "Your spell has no power over me. With the King's blood, I will be the greatest power in our realm." With a smile of pure evil on her lips,

Alona swung the dagger downward. It pierced the Blood Stone with the tip of the dagger forcing a droplet of King Ashlym's blood inside of the stone, trapping its power. Alona looked at the Queen and laughed a wicked laugh until the Blood Stone began to vibrate in her hand.

"What is happening?" Alona cried out, as the Blood Stone grew hot and began to burn her skin.

"I told you that you would never possess the power of the King's blood," Queen Privlana betrayed her amusement at seeing the horror on Alona's face.

The stone began to glow brighter than the sun as a loud, ear-piercing hum filled the room.

"Make it stop. I command you!" Alona demanded.

Queen Privlana laughed, "No power in this realm can stop this. The power of the King's blood is out of your reach forever."

Alona could no longer hold the stone as the heat grew in intensity.

Queen Privlana stood proudly and said, "Goodbye, my love; until we meet again."

With those words, the Blood Stone transformed into a ball of white flames and disappeared.

Chapter 8

Cassy sat quietly and watched the flames flicker in the fire. While she enjoyed the tale of how the Blood Key came to be, she wondered why it had chosen her. She reached up and touched the stone attached to the breastplate and felt the soft vibration again.

"Roupert, why can't I take this off?" She tugged on one of the straps going over her shoulders.

"I'm not sure, but I assume it has to do with the spell cast by Queen Privlana. The stone has chosen you, and from what I understand, it will not only break the spell cast by the Evil Queen Alona, but it will also protect the one chosen to fight against her."

Cassy looked over at Aaron and was glad he was still asleep. "He's had a long day."

"As have we all. Let us rest, for tomorrow, you will begin your quest." Roupert saw the worried expression appear on Cassy's face and prayed she would come to no harm once she battled Queen Alona.

"Do not worry; you are safe as long as you wear the sacred Breast Plate with the Blood Key."

"I hope you're right. I sure don't like the idea of fighting an evil Queen, who has dark, magical powers," Cassy groaned.

"You have nothing to fear, once you realize you have powers of your own," Roupert smiled, then he lay on his mat and pulled the blanket up around his neck.

Cassy did her best to relax and finally closed her eyes. She was not sure if she could win a battle against the Evil Queen.

As she lay there, Roupert's words replayed in her mind. *You will realize you have powers of your own.*

"What did he mean by that?" she whispered.

***

Cassy awoke to the smell of frying bacon filling the room. She sat up and stretched then looked over at the table where Aaron was eating a thick slice of bread.

"Good morning, sleepyhead," Aaron grinned as he shoved the remainder of the bread in his mouth.

Cassy stood and walked over to the table, then she sat on one of the wooden chairs. "Good morning, what smells so good?"

"I decided to cook up some salted meat for your brother. He seems to have quite a healthy appetite," Roupert smiled as he flipped the meat in the large skillet. "Would you like a cup of hot root tea?"

"Sure, I've always liked tea." Cassy held up the empty mug sitting on the table, allowing Roupert to fill it with the hot beverage.

"It tastes best with a little Valen sap," he pointed to the small pot on the table.

"Sap? You put tree sap in your tea?" Cassy scrunched her nose.

Roupert chuckled at the expression on Cassy's face. "We use the sap from Valen tree to sweeten our drinks and food. It is magnificent; try it, and you will see for yourself."

"Thanks." Cassy reached for the small pot and removed the lid. Sticking the tip of her finger in the amber substance, she then placed it on her tongue.

The expression of pleasure on Cassy's face let Roupert know she liked it. "See, I told you it was good."

"Where's Frair this morning?" Aaron asked as he reached for another piece of bread.

"He's probably down at the river. He enjoys catching fresh fanish for his breakfast."

"Fanish, what's that?" Aaron asked.

"You do not have creatures that live in the waters of your realm? Very strange," Roupert shook his head.

"Oh, you mean fish? Yeah, we have fish in our realm," Aaron laughed. "I'm glad I don't have to eat fish for breakfast."

Roupert picked up the wooden fork to put the crisply fried meat on the platter in front of Cassy and Aaron. "Eat well, for we have a long journey ahead of us."

Cassy reached out and took a piece of the meat. She brought it up to her mouth, then took a small bite. "Hey, this tastes like bacon."

Roupert looked at Cassy. "Bacon; is that what you call it where you come from? What an odd name."

Aaron grabbed a piece and shoved it into his mouth. "Yeah, but it doesn't matter what it's called. It tastes great," he grinned as he chewed on the delicious treat.

Once everyone had finished eating, they cleaned the dishes and straightened their bedding. Next, they packed food for their trip, consisting of dried meat, dried berries, and a bag full of different types of nuts and seeds.

"Is this going to be enough food for all of us?" Aaron asked.

"Yes, this will only be used should we not have time to hunt," Roupert tucked the pouches of food inside his leather pack.

"Hunt, we get to hunt? Cool, I've never hunted before." Aaron jumped to his feet with a new sense of excitement surging through him.

Roupert stared at Aaron, unsure if he had heard him correctly. "You have never hunted before, but how do you get your meat?"

"My mom gets it from the store, or she orders it from the restaurant like when we have pizza." Aaron glanced over at Roupert, wondering why he would ask such a silly question.

"So, your father does not hunt for your meat? How strange, I have never heard of such a thing. We do not have things called stores where we get our food. We either grow our food or gather it from the woods."

Cassy looked at Roupert and shook her head. "Well, I guess you don't have fast-food restaurants either?"

The expression on his face answered her question, and she could not help but laugh.

"You come from a strange realm. Once we complete this quest, you will have to tell me more about it. Come; let us leave. Do not forget your packs."

Roupert handed Cassy and Aaron each a leather pack with a blanket, mug, bowl, and a spoon tucked inside of it. They put their arms through the leather straps and let the pack hang on their backs like the backpacks they had at home.

Roupert grabbed the sheath holding his sword, and his pack then slung them over his shoulder. After looking around the hut one last time, he walked to the door with Cassy and Aaron following closely behind. As he opened the door, they heard a loud growl coming from outside. Cassy and Aaron jumped back, but Roupert merely laughed.

"Good morning, Frair. I see you are feeling well this morning," Roupert chuckled as he walked up to the dragon, who was now laughing so hard he could barely stand.

"Yes, I am. I slept well, and my stomach is full. I see our new friends are fed and rested, as well." Frair said with enthusiasm as he watched Cassy and Aaron step outside.

"Yes, they are. Our young man, Aaron, has a healthy appetite for one so small," Roupert chuckled.

"Well, my mom always says a growing boy needs to eat, so I'm just doing as told," Aaron replied playfully.

Cassy glared at Aaron then rolled her eyes. "No, the reason you eat so much is you're a pig. I've never seen anyone who can eat as much as he does."

Frair stared at Aaron with a look of confusion on his face. "I don't understand. You say your brother is a pig, but he does not look like the creatures we eat here. Do you let him eat a lot, so he will fatten for the slaughter?"

Cassy burst out laughing at the terrified look now on Aaron's face. "No, I didn't mean he was a real pig. Only that he eats like one."

"Yeah, I'm not a real pig. I'm a boy." Aaron looked at Cassy, "Dang, Sis, are trying to get me eaten?" He then looked nervously at Frair.

"Do not worry, my friend. I do not eat pigs. I much prefer fresh fanish," Frair laughed.

Cassy and Roupert both laughed at the relieved expression now on Aaron's face.

"Come, we have far to travel today," Roupert announced as he walked into the woods.

***

The group had walked for nearly two hours when they came to a broad river.

"What now? How do we get to the other side?" Cassy groaned as she sat on a fallen tree to rest her aching feet.

"Yeah, I don't see a boat," Aaron moaned as he sat next to Cassy.

Frair glanced at Cassy and Aaron with a broad grin on his face. "Who needs a boat? Cassy can get us to the other side."

Cassy jumped to her feet. "What? How am I supposed to get us to the other side?"

Frair glanced over at Roupert then back to Cassy. "She does not know, does she?"

"Know what?" Cassy groaned.

"That you have magical powers. You are the one chosen by the Blood Key, which gives the bearer magical powers. All you need to do is make the commandment, and it is so."

Cassy's gaze met Frair's, and in that instant, she realized his words were true. "Okay, here goes nothing. I command we cross the river." She closed her eyes and waited.

Laughter filled her ears as she opened her eyes and realized nothing had happened.

"I don't get it. I did what you told me to do." Cassy groaned then stomped her foot on the ground, feeling like a complete fool.

Frair and Aaron were laughing so hard neither of them could speak.

Roupert walked over to her. "You need to be a little clearer than that. Magic has rules, and one of them is you must clearly state your command. You need to say how we are to cross the river."

Cassy rolled her eyes at this foolish idea. "Fine, let me think about it for a moment."

Silence fell over the group as they waited for Cassy to cast her spell.

She reached up and placed her hand on the Blood Key, gently caressing the surface with her fingertips. "I command the fallen tree to transform into a canoe with paddles."

Everyone held their breath and waited.

Suddenly the fallen tree beneath Aaron began to shake, causing him to jump to his feet. They all watched in amazement as it slowly lifted into the air and spun three times. Then in a puff of smoke, it transformed into a sleek canoe with two paddles.

"Wow, she did it!" Aaron shouted.

"Now she needs to command it to go to the water," Roupert said in a hushed tone.

"I command you to go set on the river's edge." Cassy felt a new sense of power as she continued to caress the Blood Key unknowingly with her fingertips as it shimmered a bright red.

Transfixed by what was happening, they all watched as the canoe slowly floated over to the water's edge and came to rest on the sandy shore.

"That was so cool," Cassy said excitedly. "So, you're saying as long as I'm wearing this plate, I can do magic?"

Roupert's face suddenly took on a serious expression. "Yes, the Blood Key gives you the Gift of Magic, but only to perform that which is good. Should you try to use it for selfish reasons, the power of the Blood Key will be taken from you."

Cassy nodded her understanding. She would have to be careful not to abuse the Blood Key, or she and Aaron would find themselves trapped in the Kingdom of Walandra forever.

"Good, let us continue our quest. Frair, I would like you to fly ahead and scout the trail.

We will meet up at the Falls of Clamore for the night."

Frair nodded his understanding then spread his wings, taking flight across the river toward the mountains in the east.

"Dang, he really can fly. That is so cool," Aaron shook his head as he walked toward the canoe.

Chapter 9

Once they arrived at the other side of the river and stood on the shore, the canoe transformed back into a fallen tree.

"Why did it do that?" Cassy asked.

"Your spells only last for as long as they are needed. Once we were safely on the other side of the river and had no further need of the boat, it changed back into the log." Roupert laughed at the disappointment on Cassy's face. "Why the sad look?"

"I guess conjuring up a Jeep 4x4 is out of the question?" she grinned.

Confused by her statement, Roupert asked, "What is a Jeep 4x4?"

"It's the coolest car ever built," Aaron interrupted.

"Car; what is a car, and why would you want one? Is it some sort of wagon?" Roupert pondered.

"Yeah, sort of; I guess you can think of it as a wagon that moves by itself. You get inside of it, and it takes you to where you want to go." Cassy hoped he understood her explanation. "I just thought it would be good not to have to walk the entire way."

"I do not know what this Jeep 4x4 is you speak of, but we do not have them in Walandra.

Therefore, you cannot use your magic to make one. The magic of the Blood Key only works for things of this realm." Roupert pointed to the path leading into the woods. "Come, we have far to travel before nightfall."

***

As the three of them walked through the woods, Cassy could not help but notice the beauty of everything around her. There were unusual looking flowers with blooms that looked like little faces surrounded by petals lining the path, and rich, green-colored mossy grass covering the forest floor.

"What's that?" Cassy pointed to the small creature sitting atop a stump.

"That's a Lillient. They are woodland creatures who once served the King and Queen," Roupert answered as he waved toward the creature.

Suddenly, the creature rose into the air and with a burst of light, spread its delicate wings and flew toward Roupert, stopping in front of him.

"Good day, Sir Roupert, it is a pleasure to see you again," the Lillient said in a warm and friendly voice.

"Good day, Arianna, it is a pleasure to see you as well," Roupert bowed his head. "What brings you here today?"

Arianna briefly glanced over at Cassy and Aaron then back to Roupert. "We heard murmurings from the woodland creatures that Abigail had returned."

She turned and looked at Cassy again. "Nonetheless, this is not Abigail. What is your name, child?"

"My name is Cassy."

Arianna looked closer at Cassy then shook her head. "I ask again, what is your name, child?"

"Cassandra, my name is Cassandra."

"Excellent, one with such a lovely name should always use it," Arianna smiled.

Aaron began to laugh at the stunned expression on Cassy's face but stopped when he saw the look of displeasure appear on Arianna's face.

Arianna turned and looked directly at Aaron. "Why do you laugh, Aaron? It is not polite to find joy in one's embarrassment."

Cassy looked at Arianna and saw the playful wink letting her know she was not angry.

"I gather you are headed to face the Evil Queen Alona, am I correct?" Arianna said to Roupert.

"Yes, I believe it is time for the curse to end and free the subjects of Walandra, as well as our Queen."

"This is the wish of the Lillients as well. For far too long, we have lived under the cruel hand of Queen Alona. We have all longed for the day our Champion would appear and free us from her control."

As Roupert and Arianna spoke, Cassy found herself transfixed by the beauty of the Lillient. She was roughly twelve inches tall, and her delicate wings shimmered like polished gold and fluttered gently, keeping her in place. Cassy noticed her clothing simmered with a warm glow that seemed to surround her, and she found it to be quite mesmerizing. Arianna also wore a crown made of small flowers, which sat atop her thick red hair. She was quite beautiful, and Cassy wondered if she would get to meet more of her kind.

"Hey, it's time to go," Aaron elbowed Cassy, bringing her out of her trance.

"Okay, sorry," she grumbled, turning away from Arianna.

"I will let the others know that you have the Champion and are headed to the castle. Be safe, my friend." Arianna smiled then bowed toward Roupert.

"Thank you, and I look forward to our next meeting," Roupert bowed as well.

Arianna turned to face Cassy. "Cassandra, I want you to know I have a good feeling about you. I believe you will be the one to end the Evil Queen's reign over our Kingdom but heed my warning. Always remember evil will do everything it can to trick you. You will need to remain strong and have faith in those around you, but above all, remember to have confidence in yourself. If you remember these things, you will be triumphant."

"Thank you, Arianna, I will remember." Cassy bowed her head and then gazed at Arianna with tears forming in her eyes. She had never had anyone have so much faith in her before, and she hoped she could live up to the trust put in her now.

Arianna turned to Roupert. "I must take my leave. The Lillients will keep watch over you during your quest against Queen Alona. Should you need our assistance, you know how to summon us."

Arianna quickly glanced at Aaron and Cassy, and in a flash of light, she was gone.

"Wow, that was so awesome," Aaron said excitedly.

Cassy stood transfixed, unsure of what to say. After a few moments, she turned to face Roupert. "Do you believe I can really beat the Evil Queen? I'm just a kid. I've never done anything like this before."

Roupert knew she was frightened, and honestly, he understood her fear. Since the Evil Queen took control of Walandra, he had lived in constant fear she would discover the secret he had kept hidden deep in the woods.

"I believe in the power of the Blood Key, Cassy. If it has faith in you, then so do I," he reached out and rested his hand on her shoulder.

"Cassandra, please call me Cassandra," she said with her cheeks flushing the softest shade of red.

Roupert bowed before her. "As you wish, Cassandra; come, we still need to make it to the Falls of Clamore before nightfall," Roupert motioned for them to follow as he continued along the path.

***

They had walked for nearly an hour in complete silence when Cassy finally spoke.

"Roupert, why did Arianna call you, Sir, and then bow to you?"

Roupert had hoped the children did not notice the formality of the greeting between him and Arianna. It had been many years since anyone had referred to him in such a manner, and honestly, he did not want to have to explain it to Frair either.

"I'm not sure this is the proper time to share that information with you." He kept his head forward, unwilling to meet her questioning gaze.

"Come on, I thought we were in this thing together. How are we supposed to beat the Evil Queen if we have secrets between us?" Cassy reached out and grasped Roupert's arm.

"Yeah, I thought we were a team," Aaron added with a hint of sadness in his voice.

Realizing they would not let the question go unanswered, Roupert stopped and looked around for a place for them to rest. "Fine, why don't we stop for a while and have something to eat. I'm sure Aaron is ready for some food."

"I thought we'd never stop to eat; I'm starving," Aaron grinned as he rubbed his stomach.

"That is no surprise," Roupert laughed. "Come, let us sit and enjoy a meal, then I will tell you of how I came to know the Lillients."

***

Once they had finished their meal of dried meat and nuts, Roupert returned the pouches of food to his leather pack. Cassy sat across from Roupert anxiously waiting for him to share the story of the Lillients, and of the secret when she noticed Aaron lean against the tree behind him.

"I'm tired; I think I'll relax for a while," Aaron yawned. No sooner had he closed his eyes than he was soundly asleep.

Cassy shook her head, giggling softly. "I guess he was tired. Well, I'm not, please continue with your story."

"Let me see, where shall I begin? Before the rule of Queen Alona, I was the King's most trusted guard. Even though I was younger than many of the King's guards, I had proven myself and gained the King's confidence."

Roupert glanced away, not wanting to meet Cassy's gaze. "I will never forgive myself for not protecting him from Alona. If I had only known, maybe I could have saved him." His mind flowed back to that dreadful day.

~~~

"Roupert, the King, she has killed the King!" Dalmen cried out as he rushed to Roupert's side.

"What are you saying? The King is not dead; I was just with him. He wanted to rest, so he went to his bedchamber." Roupert studied the young guard's expression, trying to understand why he would say such a thing.

"I swear to you, the King is dead, and our Queen has been taken, hostage. She is being taken to the dungeon as we speak," Dalmen said breathlessly with tears filling his eyes.

"Quick, we must save the Queen." Roupert pulled his sword from its sheath and ran toward the stairway, which led to the underground dungeon.

Both men ran as quickly as their feet would carry them, each saying a silent prayer Queen Privlana was unharmed. As they reached the opening to the stairway, three small, winged creatures appeared, blocking their entrance to the stairs.

"Move out of our way," Roupert demanded.

"No, Sir Roupert. You are not to save the Queen this day," one of the creatures held out her hand.

"What are you saying? Why would I not save the Queen?"

The little creature flew up closer to Roupert, close to his ear. "My name is Syrea, of the Lillients. I have a message from Queen Privlana. I shall confound this other guard so we may talk."

Syrea waved her hand at Delman, causing him to fall into a trance. "You will return to your quarters and not remember seeing Sir Roupert, nor us."

Delman nodded his head, then blindly turned and walked toward the guard's quarters.

Syrea and the other Lillients took off down the corridor with their wings glowing brighter the faster they flew.

"Quick, follow us; we have no time to waste," Syrea shouted back over her shoulder.

Roupert followed the three Lillients down the corridor and into a hidden passage, which led out of the back of the castle.

"Where are you taking me?" Roupert asked as they went through the dark passageway with only the glow from the Lillients lighting their way.

"Wait, we will be there soon," Syrea then exited the passageway which led out into the forest to a narrow path through the trees.

After several minutes, they came to a small clearing, and sitting in the center of the clearing was a large golden egg.

"Is that what I think it is?" Roupert gasped as he walked toward the egg and kneeled down in front of it.

The three Lillients flew over to the egg and landed on the soft grass next to it.

"Yes, Sir Roupert, this is the child of King Ashlym and Queen Privlana. This is Prince Frair."

Roupert looked at the egg and suddenly realized what the Lillients expected of him.

"You wish that I protect the young Prince, don't you?"

Syrea nodded her head. "Yes, he must be kept from the Evil Queen. She must not know of his existence. For if she were to learn of him, she would surely kill him."

"I don't understand. How did this all come to pass?" Roupert felt as though his entire world was collapsing in around him.

Syrea then told Roupert of how Alona had tricked King Ashlym and had killed him with the

Dagger of Destiny. She also said of how Queen Privlana had come into the bedchamber and caught Alona about to force a drop of the King's blood into the Blood Stone.

"But what of our Queen, should I not try to save her?" Roupert's eyes burned with rage.

"No, before Alona was able to cast her spell, Queen Privlana transformed into her Dragon form and cast a spell herself. She cast a spell protecting the members of the Dragon family from death by turning them to stone. Then she put a protective spell on the Blood Stone so Alona could never use its power, and the power of the King's blood as her own."

Syrea looked at Roupert with sadness showing in her eyes. "Queen Privlana is now under the power of Alona. She has our Queen locked away in the Great Dungeon, trapped in her human form. Alona has cast a spell over her so she may not transform into her Dragon form, thus stripping her of her powers."

"Then again, Alona does not understand the true power of the Dragon. You see, when Queen Privlana cast a spell on the Blood Stone, and Alona forced the droplet of the King's blood into the stone with the Dagger of Destiny, she unleashed an ancient forgotten magic."

Roupert leaned in closer, not wanting to miss a word of this grand tale.

"It was the magic of love and self-sacrifice. There is no stronger magic in any realm."

While Roupert knew love and self-sacrifice were important, he did not understand what they meant as far as magic.

Seeing the confusion on his face, Syrea continued. "You see, when Queen Privlana cast her spell to prevent Alona from gaining the power of the Blood Stone, she called forth a Champion. One who would come to our realm, and through love and self-sacrifice, break the spell cast by Alona over the Kingdom. By not understanding the Queen's words, Alona believes as long as Queen Privlana remains trapped in her human form, she is safe to rule over the kingdom forever. You see, our Queen was too smart for the evil Alona."

"May I tell this part of the story? I love this part," one of the other Lillients exclaimed excitedly.

"Of course, you may, Brianna," Syrea replied with amusement in her voice.

Brianna cleared her throat then began. "Queen Privlana is truly brilliant. Before Alona forced her to transform into her human form, she tore one of the scales covering her heart. She then cast a powerful spell, sending it to the same realm where she had sent the Blood Stone. By doing this, she linked her power to the Blood Stone. Isn't that brilliant?" Brianna smiled.

Roupert was unsure of what that meant, but he nodded his head, letting her know he heard her words.

"So, now I am aware of what has happened to our King and Queen, what do you want of me?" Roupert asked them nervously.

"The Queen wishes that you protect her son. Then once he hatches, you will protect him until the day the Champion comes to break the curse set upon the kingdom," Syrea voice took on a serious tone.

Seeing the golden egg nestled in the soft, lush grass, Roupert felt a warm sense of affection fill his soul. "I will do as requested. I will protect Prince Frair until the day he may be united with his mother and the rest of his Dragon family."

"Excellent, Sir Roupert, but I have one more thing you must know. Queen Privlana has commanded you not let Prince Frair know of her or of his heritage until the curse over the kingdom is broken."

"I don't understand why he can't know of his family? Would it not be cruel to keep the knowledge of his birthright from him?" Roupert slowly shook his head.

Syrea seeing the sorrow in his eyes, reached out and gently touched him on the cheek. "The Prince must not know of his family, for fear he may try to avenge them. The heart of a Dragon is full of great passion, so to learn of the death of his father and the enslavement of his mother and his other family members would only drive him to seek revenge. He would be no match for the power of Alona, so he must believe he is alone, and there are no other dragons in our realm."

Chapter 10

Cassy sat in silence as Roupert finished sharing the tale of the day he came to be with Frair.

"How long was it before he hatched from the egg?" Cassy asked.

Roupert looked at her with amusement in his eyes. "A Dragon does not hatch like a bird. When it is time for a Dragon to come forth into this life, the shell protecting it is burnt away with its first breath."

Cassy tipped her head to the side, not understanding what Roupert meant.

"You see, when it is time for a Dragon to come forth, it cracks a small hole in the shell with one of its talons. Then as air fills the egg, the Dragon takes its first breath and blows forth fire, which burns the shell and releases it. Do you understand now?"

Cassy nodded her head with sorrow showing on her face. "So, you lived alone waiting for him to come forth from the egg? That's so sad."

"I was not always alone as I waited for the day of Frair's birth. I had our friends the Lillients and other woodland creatures for company. Then I had the joy of getting to know your great-grandmother, Abigail." His eyes revealed the longing in his heart.

Roupert jumped to his feet, not wanting to continue this conversation. "Come, it grows late, and Frair will worry if we do not join him soon."

Realizing there was no need to pursue the subject of her great-grandmother at this time, Cassy stood. "Come on, Aaron, wake up; he's going to leave us behind if we don't hurry."

***

"What took you so long? I was beginning to worry," Frair huffed as he stacked the last of the wood next to the fire.

"I am sorry, but we stopped to eat, and time got away from us," Roupert grinned as he saw the disappointed look on Frair's face.

"I hope you are still hungry. I have fanish roasting over the fire, and I found some sweet berries," Frair retorted with a hint of irritation in his voice.

"I'm hungry, Frair," Aaron licked his lips. "Those look great. I've never had fish cooked that way. Fish and berries for dinner sound delicious."

"So, in your realm, they are called fish?" Frair grinned. "What a strange word."

Frair walked over to the fire and lifted the fish away from the direct flames. "They are ready to eat."

Aaron reached for one of the sticks with a cooked fish, and then took a few steps away from the fire before he sat on the sand to eat.

Frair grabbed one of the sticks and handed it to Cassy. "Here you go; you need to keep up your strength."

"Thank you, Frair. As a matter of fact, I am hungry," she smiled. She took the stick with the fish, then walked over to Aaron and sat next to him.

"This is really good," Aaron moaned with delight as he shoved another bite of the fish in his mouth.

"Frair, you may need to cook some more fish. It looks like our young friend is hungry this evening," Roupert chuckled as he watched Aaron take another bite.

Frair looked at Aaron and shook his head. "Well, at least, I know all my work will not go to waste. Here, try the berries with the fish. It is quite tasty."

Frair set a sizeable bowl-shaped leaf filled with berries in front of Aaron and Cassy. Aaron carefully examined the berries before he scooped up a handful and shoved them in his mouth.

"They're delicious. They taste like strawberries," Aaron grinned as he chewed the sweet berries.

Roupert and Frair each took a stick with a cooked fish and sat across from Cassy and Aaron. As they enjoyed their feast, they all laughed and shared funny stories of their lives. In spite of this, there was an unspoken apprehension hovering over the group at the thought of facing the Evil Queen Alona.

***

The moon shone brightly on the water as it flowed over the rocks into the deep pool below.

The Falls of Clamore are quite beautiful, Cassy thought to herself.

As she lay by the fire, she could not help but wonder what lies ahead for her.

How am I supposed to win a battle against the Evil Queen? I'm just a kid. Why do they believe I can break the curse and free the kingdom? The words burned in Cassy's mind. She wanted to believe she was the Champion that all the subjects of Walandra had long-awaited, but a voice inside of her mind kept reminding her she was just a silly teenager.

Turning on her side, she struggled to get comfortable. "I sure do miss my bed."

Not able to fall asleep, Cassy decided to get up and add more wood to the fire. She walked over to the stack of wood when suddenly she noticed a small light floating along the water's edge.

"What's that?" she whispered to herself.

The light flickered as it began to float up and down, then it stopped and started to move slowly along the shoreline again.

Cassy tossed a piece of wood on the fire then walked toward the mysterious light, wondering what it could be. She glanced over her shoulder at the three sleeping forms by the fire then she continued toward the light.

"Stop, wait, who are you?" Cassy whispered as she rushed after the light.

Once she was a distance from the campsite, the light stopped and then transformed into its true form as it waited for her to approach.

"Arianna, is that you?" Cassy asked as she closed the distance between them.

"Yes, it is I, Cassandra. I wanted to speak to you in private. Please sit so we may talk." Arianna waved her hand, and a small wooden bench appeared.

Cassy sat on the bench, then Arianna sat beside her. A few tense moments passed between them before Arianna finally spoke. "I sensed your fear as you lie by the fire, trying to sleep."

"Yeah, I'm a bit worried, Arianna. How am I supposed to conquer the Evil Queen? I don't know anything about magic, let alone how to properly use it. What if I mess up? What if I'm unable to do what I'm supposed to do?" Cassy hung her head and softly cried.

"Cassandra, the Blood Key chose you for a reason. It saw strength in you; otherwise, it never would have brought you here. Then again, you will need to force your fears aside and believe in yourself. For you see, Queen Alona will use any doubts or fears you have against you."

"I just don't feel brave enough to do what's asked of me. May I ask you a question?" Cassy looked at Arianna through tear-filled eyes.

"Of course, you may," Arianna assured her.

"When we first got here, Frair thought I was my great-grandmother returning to save the people of Walandra. When was she here?"

Arianna sat for a moment, remembering those troubled days.

"The spirits were low among the subjects of the kingdom when Abigail came to us. She appeared to me, and the other Lillients, confused and afraid. We knew immediately why she had come, as she wore the sacred Dragon's Breast Plate with the Blood Key; the very one you wear now." Arianna pointed at the plate on Cassy's chest.

"I don't understand why it would choose me, though. I've never done anything brave my entire life," Cassy moaned as she rubbed her hand along the edge of the plate.

"Silly child, the Blood Key did not choose you for your past deeds. It chose you for your inner strength. I have looked into your soul, and I see greatness there. You may not know it yet, but you possess much strength and a willingness to sacrifice for the greater good. That is what drew the Blood Key to you. Those are also the very things that brought the Blood Key to your great-grandmother."

Cassy shook her head, still not willing to accept her fate.

"Arianna, I have another question. What is it I have to do to defeat the Evil Queen and restore the kingdom?"

Arianna could see the doubt and fear in Cassy's eyes, but she also knew she must know what they expected of her to prepare for the task ahead. The Lillients had made that mistake with Abigail, so she did not want to repeat it.

"As you know on that fateful day when Alona cursed the kingdom, our Queen Privlana also cast a spell. Yet, Alona, in her blind quest for power, did not understand what our Queen had done.

When she cast her spell on the Blood Stone, she transformed it into a unique key."

Cassy nodded her understanding as Arianna continued.

"And through that spell, the Blood Key would only come to one who was worthy, one who would only use its power for the benefit of the Kingdom. That is why the stone burned the hand of Alona before it vanished. The spell cast on it by Queen Privlana sent the Blood Key to a realm where Alona could not find it."

Arianna shook her head as the painful memories of that day consumed her. "This, of course, angered Alona significantly, so she cast our Queen into the Great Dungeon, where she stays trapped in her human form today. Still, our Queen was much too smart for Alona. Before changing into her weaker human form, Queen Privlana cast a spell on the Dragon scale over her heart. The spell joined the scale with the Blood Key to be worn by the champion when they came to Walandra to battle the evil Alona."

"You mean to say this same plate I wear is from the Queen? Roupert had said it, but I didn't honestly believe him." Cassy's eyes were wide with surprise.

"Yes, my child. That is why you must have faith in yourself. The scale that covers a Dragon's heart has magical qualities, and it would never come to someone not worthy. You have two powerful objects that have chosen you for an important task."

"Okay, but what is that task. What am I supposed to do?"

"You need to return the Breast Plate to Queen Privlana with the Blood Key. Once the Breast Plate is returned, the curse will be broken, and Alona will be destroyed."

Cassy suddenly felt a knot tighten in her stomach. "Okay, so let me see if I understand this completely. I need to go to the castle and somehow make my way to the dungeon. Then once I'm there, I must return the Breast Plate with the Blood Key to Queen Privlana without the Evil Queen stopping me. Sure, that doesn't sound like a problem at all."

"Do not question your abilities, Cassandra. I have faith that you will fulfill your destiny."

"I don't understand something. When Aaron and I first appeared to Frair, he mentioned that he believed I was Abigail, returning to complete her quest. What happened? Why didn't she beat Alona when she was here?"

Arianna closed her eyes, remembering that dreadful day.

"Abigail was actually brave, and she fought well against the Evil Queen Alona, only she made the mistake of trusting someone who was not pure of heart."

"I don't understand. Who did she put her trust in?"

"I blame myself for not warning her, but he was cunning and convinced her she must battle the Queen alone." The look of sadness in Arianna's eyes told Cassy it was a painful memory and one she wanted to prevent happening again.

"What happened?"

"He led her into a trap. Abigail had no way of knowing several of Alona guards lay in wait to attack when she entered the dungeon holding our Queen. She fought bravely, but she was no match for the guards."

"Oh no," Cassy cried out.

Arianna saw the fear in Cassy's eyes as she continued. "They had her trapped against a wall and were about to strike her down when the Blood Key began to glow a fiery red. Queen Privlana had fought against her chains, trying to help Abigail, but she was helpless to save her. Then just as one of the guards moved in to strike Abigail down, she vanished."

Cassy sat up straight, her eyes wild with fear. "Oh my, what happened to her? Is that when she was returned home?"

"Yes, the Blood Key returned her to her realm. You see, the spell Queen Privlana had initially cast protected Abigail from death, as the Blood Key and sacred Breast Plate will do for you. This is why you must return it to our Queen. If Abigail were to have died at the hands of Alona's guards, Alona would have gotten the power of the Blood Key as her own."

Cassy ran her finger across the Blood Key, feeling its warmth.

"Is it the drop of the King's blood that gives it its power?" Cassy asked.

"Yes, King Ashlym was very powerful. There was no stronger magic in all of our realm. That is why Alona wanted to possess his power by forcing it inside of the Blood Stone."

"I still don't know if I can beat the Evil Queen, but I will do my best." Cassy tried to muster the courage she knew she would need to face this quest.

Arianna whispered softly. "That is all we can ask of you. Come, you need your rest for tomorrow will be a strenuous day."

Arianna spread her wings, then flew up and gently touched Cassy on the forehead. "This will help you rest."

"Thank you, goodnight," Cassy stood, wondering if she would be able to do everything expected of her.

"Summon me should you need to talk or have any more questions, and I will come. I have enjoyed our time together, Cassandra."

In a flash of light, Arianna and the wooden bench disappeared.

Cassy returned to the fire, where the others were still sleeping soundly. She walked back over to her blanket and lay on the ground. As Cassy pulled the blanket around her shoulders, she noticed how she was suddenly exhausted.

"That was a neat trick, Arianna," Cassy yawned as she closed her eyes and drifted off to sleep.

Chapter 11

"Good morning, sleepyhead," Aaron laughed as he watched Cassy stand and rub the sleep from her eyes.

"Good morning," Cassy groaned. "I sure hope some of that root tea is ready."

"As a matter of fact, it is. I even brought some Valen sap to go in it," Roupert smiled as he reached for the kettle hanging over the fire.

Cassy reached into her pack and pulled out her mug as he filled it with the warm liquid then poured some of the sap into it.

"Thank you, I need this," Cassy grinned, then she took a sip of the tea. "I could get used to this stuff."

"Not me, I'd rather have a glass of chocolate milk," Aaron made a sour face.

Frair shot Aaron a confused look. "What is chocolate milk? Is it a liquid from a beast? What do they look like?"

Aaron and Cassy exchanged glances and began to laugh.

"I do not understand what is so funny," Frair protested.

"Chocolate is a sweet substance. It's a candy that is melted and added to milk from cows," Cassy snickered, trying to control her laughter.

"I do not understand why you must add something sweet to your milk. Do your cows, as you call them, not make good tasting milk?" Frair still did not understand why someone would add anything to milk.

"It just makes the milk taste better," Aaron said playfully.

"Well, if you do not like the root tea, there is plenty of water to drink," Roupert pointed toward the waterfalls. "We do need to remember to fill our water pouches before we leave."

"Cassy, there's some fruit here for breakfast. Roupert and I went out and picked it while you were sleeping. It's pretty good. Those purple ones taste like peaches, and the pink ones taste like pears," Aaron grinned as he took another bite of one of the purple fruits.

"Thanks, but I think I'll just sit here and enjoy my root tea while I wake up," Cassy groaned.

"Do not take too long to wake up, we have a long way yet to go," Roupert winked. "Maybe you should have gone to sleep sooner."

"Yeah, I'll be sure to do that tonight." Cassy wondered if Roupert knew of her talk with Arianna, but she did not want to bring it up in case he did not know. "Maybe I'll have one of those purple ones. I'd hate to have to eat that dried stuff again."

Once everyone had finished their breakfast, they doused the fire, and then put their blankets and mugs back into their packs.

"Okay, let us continue on our journey," Roupert announced.

Everyone gathered their gear and followed Roupert along the water's edge.

***

Cassy found the breathtaking beauty of Walandra incredible. From the crystal blue waters of the Falls of Clamore to the tall green trees of the dense forest. This Kingdom indeed was a wondrous place. Occasionally, as they walked along the trail, she would see a curious woodland creature, peering from behind a tree or from under a toadstool. She wondered if they knew who she was and if they expected her to defeat the Evil Queen Alona, as well.

"Roupert, I'm tired, can we take a short break?" Cassy groaned as she sat on a rock next to a tall tree. She then pulled her water pouch from her pack.

"Have you tired already?" Frair teased.

"Yeah, we haven't been walking that long," Aaron added.

Cassy glared at Frair and Aaron with an annoyed expression on her face before she stuck her tongue out at them.

"I guess you have your answer," Roupert laughed. "Let us take some time to relax. I'm thirsty as well."

After taking a drink of water, Cassy leaned back against the tree and closed her eyes. It felt good to relax and have time to clear her mind when suddenly…

"What the heck?" she cried out.

The rock beneath her began to move, rolling from side to side until it finally tossed her to the ground.

"My goodness, didn't anyone teach you it's not polite to sit on someone?"

Cassy rolled over and looked into the eyes of the offended creature.

"Yes, no, I mean..." her words caught in her throat.

The creature stood on his four short legs and shook. "Well, which is it?"

Cassy crawled toward Roupert. "I thought you were a rock. I didn't know..."

"Pomram, stop picking on her," Roupert laughed as he helped Cassy to her feet.

"Cool, he looks like an armadillo, just like the ones we have back home," Aaron pointed toward Pomram.

"Armadillo, what is this armadillo?" Pomram asked.

"An armadillo is an animal that has armor on its back for protection. They're really neat." Aaron stepped closer to Pomram for a better look.

"These armadillo's sound interesting. Do you go around sitting on them also?" Pomram asked with a hint of sarcasm in his voice.

Cassy had heard enough. "No, we don't, but they don't look like a rock either. I'm sorry I sat on you. I never meant any disrespect. I was just tired and wanted to rest for a few moments."

Pomram looked up at Cassy. "Okay, no harm was done." He then glanced at Roupert, and they both began to laugh.

"What? What's so funny," Cassy groaned.

"You should have seen your face once you realized I was not a rock. I have to admit I thought your eyes were going to pop out of your face," Pomram laughed so hard he could barely stand.

"I know. it took everything I had not to laugh," Roupert chuckled.

"Her face was rather amusing," Frair teased.

"Fine, go ahead and laugh at my expense, but I'll get even."

"Oh man, you guys are in big trouble. The last thing you want is Cassy upset with you," Aaron grinned.

The three of them looked at Cassy with concerned expressions on their faces.

"I think we need to get going," Roupert said when he saw Aaron and Frair nod their agreement.

"It was nice to meet you, Cassy and Aaron. I hope we will get to visit again." Pomram hoped she was not still upset with him.

"It was nice to meet you," Aaron waved his hand as he walked toward Roupert.

Cassy walked toward Pomram, then leaned down and gently stroked the top of his head. "I'm glad we met, too, and I promise not to sit on you the next time we meet."

Pomram peered up at Cassy, with his cheeks flushed a bright red. "Maybe it wouldn't be so bad, now that we are friends."

Cassy laughed softly and then bent down and kissed Pomram on the forehead. "Goodbye."

"Come on, Cassy; we're burning daylight," Aaron shouted as he disappeared into the trees with Roupert and Frair.

***

The group had walked for nearly another hour when they came to an old wooden bridge suspended over a deep ravine.

"Stop, who goes there?" a croaky voice came from the bushes next to the bridge.

"It is I, Roupert. I wish access to cross your bridge."

"What is your purpose? Why do you need to cross my bridge?"

"I travel with the one who has come to do battle with Queen Alona," Roupert announced in a firm voice.

"You are with the one who is to remove the curse and restore the Kingdom of Walandra to its once glory?" The voice now spoke with enthusiasm.

Roupert glanced at Cassy then smiled. "Yes, she wears the sacred Breast Plate with the Blood Key."

"Step forward, so I may see you," the voice now grew soft and welcoming.

Cassy hesitated, giving Roupert a concerned look when she took two steps forward.

"It is you; praise be. We have waited for many years." The bushes began to rustle, when suddenly a small man appeared, holding his cap in his hands. "What is your name?"

Cassy looked at the man and smiled. "My name is Cassandra."

"That is a beautiful name for a lovely young lady. I am honored to meet you, Cassandra." The man bowed his head.

Roupert stepped forward and held out his hand. "It is good to see you again, Othan."

Othan took the offered hand and returned the handshake. "As it is to see you again, my friend," he then turned to Frair.

"Hello, my Dragon friend. You haven't set any fires lately, have you?" Othan teased.

"No, but Roupert doesn't let me sleep inside the hut anymore," Frair winked playfully.

"That is wise of him," Othan responded.

Othan walked over to Cassy. He then reached out and took her hand in his. "I feel great courage in this one, even though she questions herself. The Blood Key has chosen well."

Cassy was unsure of what to say.

Aaron stepped forward and faced Othan. "Can you see if I'm brave too?"

Othan turned toward Aaron. "Ah, give me your hand."

Aaron held out his hand to Othan, who grasped it with his. "Let me see… hmmm… you, my blue-eyed friend, are quite intelligent, but you do not seem to apply yourself. I see a great future ahead of you, but only if you take the time to fully understand what is going on around you before you act."

Aaron pulled his hand away, wondering what Othan had meant. He knew he was smart, but the other part made no sense to him.

"Thanks," he replied with less than an enthusiastic tone in his voice.

Othan turned back to Roupert with a grave expression on his face. "There has been much talk among the woodland creatures of the arrival of the Champion to battle the Evil Queen Alona. You must take heed as word has without a doubt reached the Queen, and she is preparing. We must not allow her to best our Champion again."

As Cassy listened to Othan, she wondered if she would be able to win against the Evil Queen. She reached up and rubbed her fingertips along the Blood Key, feeling the warmth radiating from it.

"It talks to you, does it not?" Othan's voice took on a serious tone.

"Huh? Ah, I'm not sure," Cassy quickly pulled her hand away from the Blood Key and put it down to her side.

Othan reached up and touched the Blood Key. "You must trust the great power that is living inside the Blood Key. The King's blood is mighty, and if you believe in it and yourself, there is no force in this realm or any other that can stop you in your quest. The spell cast by our Queen Privlana will protect you, but you must believe. I see greatness in you, Cassandra. I only pray you can accept your destiny."

"Do you really think I can do it? I'm so scared I will fail," she turned her head, not wanting to meet his gaze.

"Come close, child," Othan motioned for her to kneel down in front of him. "I believe in the wisdom of the Blood Key and the King's blood hidden within. I believe it chose you because you have a rare gift, the gift of courage and self-sacrifice. You may not believe in your destiny yet, but soon you will learn why you were chosen as our Champion."

Cassy did not know what to say. Intense emotions surged through her body, and she struggled not to cry.

"Thank you, Othan. Thank you for believing in me." She reached out and hugged Othan so tightly she lifted him from the ground.

"Oh, my, please put me down, Cassandra," Othan gasped, surprised by this unexpected show of affection.

Cassy quickly set Othan down on the ground. "I'm sorry, I never meant…"

Othan straightened his ruffled clothes then gazed up into her eyes. "There is no need to apologize. I must say I rather enjoyed it."

"I enjoyed it too." Cassy saw compassion shining in Othan's eyes. She had to admit in spite of his ruff-n-gruff exterior, Othan was, in fact, a gentle soul.

Roupert stepped forward and patted Othan on the shoulder. "My old friend, you need to be careful. One might begin to think you are a pushover for such a lovely young lady."

Othan turned toward Roupert. "That is no surprise, Roupert. I have always had a soft place in my heart for pretty young ladies. Especially when they are those such as our Cassandra here," he glanced over at Cassy and winked.

"Well, my old friend, we have far to travel today, so we must continue on our way. It is always good to see you," Roupert winked.

"Wait, before you go, I have something for Cassandra." Othan turned and quickly walked over to the bridge. As suddenly as he had appeared, he disappeared behind the bush where he had first appeared. After a couple of minutes, he returned and was holding a small glass vial. He held out his hand and offered it to Cassy.

Cassy took the offered object and held it up, examining it carefully. "What is it?"

"It is the nectar from the blossom of the Samen plant. It is a very particular plant, as it only blooms once every twenty years, and then you must capture the nectar from the heart of the blossom in the light of the full moon."

Cassy's eyes grew wide with amazement as she watched the fluid inside of the vial slowly swirl and change its color from blue to purple then back to blue. "What's it supposed to do?"

"It will provide you your greatest need," Othan replied flatly.

"I don't understand. When will I know?" Cassy shook her head, not convinced if she understood him.

"You will know when you need it, and when you do, open the vial and drink it all."

Othan reached up and touched her hand. "But be forewarned. Do not use it for personal gain, for if you do, what happens next will be very grave.

The nectar of the bloom is sacred, so you must only use it in a time of extreme need. Do you understand?" Othan looked Cassy deeply in the eyes, letting her know the importance of his words.

Cassy nodded her understanding, then she reached for the pack on her back.

"No, do not put the vial in your pack. It must be kept in a safe place where you can get it without delay." Othan raised his hand, and with one finger, he touched the Breast Plate. Suddenly the Plate began to vibrate, and in an instant, a small opening appeared near the Blood Key.

"Hand me the vial, please." Othan held out his hand.

Cassy placed the vial in Othan's outstretched hand, and then she watched as he put the vial into the opening, he then tapped twice on the Blood Key. Once he pulled his hand away, the small opening holding the vial had vanished.

"Where did it go?" Cassy cried out.

"It is hidden safely within the Breast Plate where no one can take it from you," Othan smiled.

"But how do I get it out when I need it?" Cassy looked down at the place where it had vanished and ran her finger along the smooth surface.

Othan shook his head and laughed. "Were you not paying attention? Here," Othan reached up and tapped the center of the Blood Key twice, and when he pulled his hand away, the opening appeared with the vial safely secured inside.

"Oh, I get it now. I tap the center of the Blood Key twice to open and close it; cool," she grinned.

Othan looked at Cassy, confused by her response. "I do not understand. It is not cold. Why do you say it is cold?"

Cassy could not hold back her laughter. "No, I didn't mean it was cold. That's just a figure of speech. In my realm, when you say something is cool, it means it's good."

Othan shook his head, unsure of the strange customs of this realm she came from. "I see, well, I guess it is cool to have met you today, Cassandra."

"It is cool to have met you too," Cassy teased while the rest of the group broke out into laughter.

Roupert reached out and rested his hand on Othan's shoulder. "It is time for us to leave, my old friend."

Othan's eyes gazed into Cassy's with sadness clearly showing in them. "Please remember to use the nectar should you find yourself facing a challenging time against the Evil Queen. If you drink it with purity of heart, you will receive that which you need to be triumphant over her dark magic."

Cassy reached up and rested her hand above the glass vial hidden inside of the Breast Plate, feeling a warm sensation under her fingertips. "Thank you, Othan, I will remember.

Frair walked over to Cassy and took her hand in his. "You will not go against Queen Alona alone. I will stay by your side, no matter what the future holds."

Cassy could see the compassion burning in Frair's bright green eyes. "Thank you, that means a lot to me."

"Hey, I'll be there with you too," Aaron chimed in. "There is no way I'm gonna let some wicked Queen do anything to my sister."

The determined expression on Aaron's face made Othan chuckle, "It sounds like your brother is a brave warrior as well. Queen Alona will inevitably be defeated by two such fierce warriors standing by your side."

Frair and Aaron felt pride as they held their heads up high.

"The Evil Queen will soon face her demise," Frair growled, with Aaron nodding in agreement.

Cassy was glad to have Frair and Aaron with her. She glanced up at Roupert and noticed the pride in his eyes. "Thank you all. I'm so pleased you are here with me."

Roupert reached out and gently touched her on the cheek. As their gazes locked, he could see Abigail's face staring back at him with the memories of the time they had spent together, flooding back into his mind.

"Are you okay?" Cassy asked, seeing the emotions escaping from the safe place in his heart where Roupert had kept them safely hidden.

"Ah, yes, I am fine. Come, we must go." Roupert cleared his throat, then he walked toward the bridge with the others following closely behind.

"Goodbye, my friends," Othan called out, as they crossed the bridge.

"Goodbye," they all waved back to him, and then they disappeared into the woods on the other side.

Chapter 12

The woods seemed to grow exceptionally dense and dark, as the group got further away from the bridge and Othan.

"Dang, it's creepy here," Aaron groaned as he looked around at the tall trees that seemed to be closing in on them.

Frair looked at Aaron, confused by this statement. "What is creepy?"

"It means scary. Somewhere you don't want to be," Aaron grinned nervously.

Frair looked around at the trees. "Yes, it is creepy here, but if you stay close to me, I'll protect you."

Cassy watched the conversation between her little brother and the young dragon and realized this was something no one at home would ever believe. She was glad they had met Frair and Roupert, for she knew she did not want to face the Evil Queen alone.

"Well, I hope you two are going to protect me," Cassy teased.

Frair and Aaron exchanged glances, feeling confident in their ability to protect Cassy.

"We will be by your side, but you are the Champion. The Blood Key has chosen you, which gives you the power to conquer the Queen," Frair said with reverence.

Taken aback by the statement, Cassy was at a loss for what to say. She knew she was supposed to be the chosen Champion, but she had never completely understood what it meant. At seeing the look of innocence and trust on their faces, she suddenly felt the enormity of what she was facing, this causing fear and doubt to consume her entire being.

"Cassy, are you alright?" Roupert asked, seeing the emotions surging through her.

Cassy wanted to scream, *NO,* and run away, but where would she go? She finally steadied her nerves before answering him. "I'm fine. I was just thinking about what's ahead for us, that's all."

Roupert understood her concern, for he was experiencing the same fear. Would she finally bring about the fall of Queen Alona and restore the Dragon rule over the Kingdom of Walandra? As he gazed at Cassy, he again saw Abigail looking back at him.

Stop, you must not let your heart go to that place, he silently scolded himself.

They all walked without speaking until the sound of Aaron's stomach grumbling broke the silence.

"Dang, I'm hungry," he laughed as he patted his stomach.

"I can see you are," Roupert teased. "Why don't we stop here and eat before our young friend here fades away from starvation."

"I smell some berries nearby. I will go and get some for us," Frair offered.

"May I come with you?" Cassy asked.

Frair looked at Roupert, who nodded his approval. "Yes, I would enjoy your company."

"Aaron and I will wait here for you. Now don't take too long, or Aaron may find me to be a tasty treat," Roupert laughed as he lightly punched Aaron on the shoulder.

"Come, the berries are this direction," Frair waved for Cassy to follow him into the thick trees.

***

Cassy followed Frair as he weaved through the trees until they came to a small clearing.

"Look, they're over there," he pointed to the berry bushes on the other side of the clearing.

They quickly crossed the small grassy grove to the thick berry bushes growing in the bright sunlight.

"It's nice here," Cassy glanced around.

"Yes, it's not creepy, right?" Frair teased playfully.

"It's definitely not creepy," Cassy agreed.

It had amazed Cassy how things seemed to grow in such abundance in Walandra. There were bright colored flowers, lining the trees-edge, and the berry bushes were so full of fruit she wondered how the branches held them without breaking. She reached for one of the berries then stopped when something caught her eye. "What the heck is that?"

Frair turned to look where Cassy was pointing. "I don't see anything other than berries."

Cassy stepped back. "You can't see that?"

Frair looked at the bush again, where she had pointed. "No, only berries. Are you feeling alright?"

"The dragon cannot see me. I am here for you, so only you may see me," the little creature said as it stepped out of the bush into the light.

Cassy looked at the creature then back to Frair, who now seemed frozen in time. "What have you done to Frair?"

"He is unharmed. In his mind, you are both picking berries and having a wonderful time. My name is Keira, and I wanted to introduce myself."

Cassy marveled at the beauty of the tiny creature. Her hair was the color of fine-spun gold and her eyes the color of the sky on a summer's day. She was only six inches tall and wore a dress made of a substance as delicate as butterfly wings.

"What are you, and why are you here?" Cassy asked.

"I am a Milif. We are beings sent to watch over those who have an important purpose of fulfilling. Queen Privlana prayed I watch over you and see you remain safe as you continue on your quest. I have been with you since you arrived in our realm."

Cassy looked carefully at Keira, trying to gage her honesty.

"You do not know if you can trust me. I assure you that you can, but I am glad you are not quick to trust. You have many dangers ahead of you, so you will need to believe your heart." Keira reached out and touched Cassy's hand.

"I feel much strength and courage churning inside of you. Never doubt yourself, and always remember I am with you. Now, I must go. The others are waiting for you and Frair to return with the berries, but first..." Keira raised her tiny arm and waved it in the air, making a basket full of berries appear on the ground at Cassy's feet.

Cassy looked down at basket overflowing with juicy berries. "We didn't have a basket when we came here. How do I explain the basket?"

"Do not fear. Frair will remember finding the basket next to the bush," Keira quipped playfully.

Cassy shook her head in amazement, wondering what other things Keira had done since her arrival in the Kingdom of Walandra.

"Thank you, I know we'll enjoy them," Cassy said.

Keira smiled, and in a flash of light, she vanished.

"Come on, we've picked enough to feed an army," Frair said as he lifted the basket. "I hope whoever left this here doesn't mind us borrowing it."

"I'm sure they won't mind," Cassy grinned as she followed Frair back across the clearing.

***

"Wow, that was fast," Aaron said as he saw Cassy and Frair come out of the thick trees, holding the basket filled with berries.

"Where did you find a basket?" Rouper asked, unsure if he liked the idea of someone being anywhere close to them.

Frair walked over to where Roupert and Aaron had spread out the dried meat, and the nuts and seeds on a blanket.

"It was sitting next to the berry bushes, so we sort of borrowed it," Frair answered sheepishly.

Roupert looked at Frair with a look of disappointment on his face. "Well, after we are finished eating, you will return the basket to where you found it."

Realizing Roupert was not pleased with him, Frair hung his head in shame. "I'm sorry. I will return it."

"Don't be too hard on him. The basket is old and probably forgotten there a long time ago. Look, it's barely holding together." Cassy pointed at the basket, which appeared old and worn where just moments before it was in perfect condition.

"That basket is not old," Roupert said, but then he realized he was mistaken. "Strange, I could have sworn it was in perfect condition."

"Well, I don't care if it's old or new, I'm starving." Aaron reached into the basket and shoved a handful into his mouth.

Realizing there is no need to worry about the basket any longer, Roupert reached for the berries, "These do look delicious."

While the four of them sat on the blanket, enjoying their meal, Cassy thought back to her conversation with Keira and wondered what lay ahead for them as they got closer to the castle of Queen Alona.

Chapter 13

"What do you mean another Champion has arrived? That is impossible!"

Queen Alona had believed she was safe from another Champion coming to the Kingdom of Walandra.   After Abigail had returned to her realm, Alona had cast a repelling spell around the kingdom to prevent another Champion from coming to complete the task of destroying her rule.

"I'm sorry, my Queen, but it is true.   The Champion is traveling to the castle as we speak," the guard said nervously.

Queen Alona was not pleased with the news of a Champion arriving to challenge her rule. She looked at the guard, who now backed away, but before he could make his escape, she lifted her hand and turned the terrified man into a pile of ash on the stone floor.

"I will not be threatened by a mere child," the Queen roared as she rushed from the room, scattering the pile of ash across the floor with the hem of her dress.

***

Flickering torches lit the dark stairway leading down to the dungeon. As Queen Alona reached the last step, she stopped for a moment to take in the scene before her.

In the corner of the vast room was Queen Privlana. She sat on a filthy mat in worn-out clothes, trapped in her human form by the cursed chain attached to the dungeon wall.

She looked up and saw Alona standing at the base of the stairs. "Hello Alona, what brings you to see me today?"

Alona did not care for the informal way Privlana referred to her. She squared her shoulders then slowly walked toward the once-great Queen Privlana, Queen of the Dragon Clan.

"How small you look trapped in your human form. To see you living in such a manner; brings joy to my heart," Alona said with sarcasm dripping from each word.

"Enjoy this time while you can," Privlana replied defiantly.

Alona stepped closer and looked Privlana directly in the eyes. "You know, don't you?"

"What could I possibly know? You have me trapped in this dungeon, away from everything I hold dear," Privlana taunted.

Alona felt anger and fear churn up from deep inside of her. She knew to be in her human form had weakened Privlana's powers, but she also knew there were forces in Walandra forever faithful to the Dragon Queen.

Alona threateningly raised her arm. "Do not toy with me, Privlana. I will cast you into the Land of Shadows where you will suffer for all eternity."

Privlana began to laugh. "You do not have the power to cast me anywhere. You may have me imprisoned in this dungeon, but you cannot send me to the Land of Shadows. I am of the Dragon Clan, and your power over me is limited."

Alona felt her face flush red with rage. She knew Privlana was correct. Her powers were limited, but once she had control of the Blood Stone, all that would change.

"I may not be able to send you to the Land of Shadows, but I sent your beloved husband there," Alona laughed when she saw the sadness appear in Privlana's eyes.

Privlana reached down and touched the leg cuff, holding the chain to her ankle. "Enjoy these last days of your rule over the subjects of Walandra, Alona. For soon, you will meet your end. This chain protects you from my wrath, but the Champion is coming, and she will release me from this bondage. Then once I'm free…"

Hate burned in Alona's eyes as she stepped forward, her body quivering with rage. "Quiet You will never be free from that chain. I will rule over this kingdom forever!"

Queen Privlana's gaze met Alona's, and for an instant, both found themselves trapped inside each other's minds.

Alona fell back then she cried out while holding her hands to her temples. She then turned toward Privlana with an expression of pure amusement on her face. "So, you think you're so clever, but your heart betrays you."

A new fear consumed Privlana, as she realized her thoughts had betrayed her.

"Your son, he comes with the Champion. Yes, it was clever to have the Lillients take the egg containing the young Prince away from the castle to protect him from the curse. I wonder, does he know of his heritage? Does he know of his Royal Bloodline, but more importantly, does he know of his powers?"

Sensing Privlana's fear, Alona continued, "He doesn't know, does he?" Alona smirked when she saw the confirmation in Privlana's eyes.

Alona rubbed her hands together. "Yes, this can be fortuitous for my plan."

"Your evil will never win over the new Champion. She has a strong spirit and will defeat you," Privlana cried out with shame for allowing Alona to see into her heart. She had managed to keep the secret of Frair for all these long and lonely years, but in her excitement, she had allowed Alona to learn of his existence.

Alona saw the fear in Privlana's eyes, and she suddenly felt a new sense of power surge through her. "Before learning of your son, I must admit I was worried, but now…"

"Do not harm my son," Privlana cried out.

Alona scowled, "I have no intention of hurting the young Prince. In fact, I plan to welcome him with open arms and love in my heart."

Privlana was not sure if she had heard correctly. "What do you plan to do?"

"What I have planned for the young Prince is not your concern. Just let it be known, he will provide the power I need to destroy any hold you or anyone has on the subjects of Walandra, once and for all." Alona spun on her heel and quickly walked to the staircase.

"Alona, no, please do not do this," Privlana pleaded.

Alona stopped at the base of the stairway and then turned to face Privlana, "Thank you for the informative visit, but I must go make preparations for the return of the young Prince."

She then vanished up the stairway, leaving a chorus of laughter floating on air.

***

The sun sat low in the sky as the group exited the thick woods.

"Jeez, I'm glad to be out of there," Aaron groaned.

"What's the matter? Do you not like the forest?" Frair teased.

"I don't mind the forest. It's all the strange things watching us," Aaron grinned nervously.

Frair nodded his head in agreement. "Yes, many eyes are watching us."

Roupert glanced at the two young boys and could not help but smile. "Come, my brave warriors. It grows late. Let us set up camp and rest. Tomorrow, we will arrive at the castle, so we need to make our final preparations before we confront the Evil Queen Alona."

Frair and Aaron felt a cold chill move over their bodies at the thought of facing the Evil Queen.

"Come, Aaron, let's gather wood for the fire." Frair hoped this task would help to shake the feeling of dread consuming his entire being.

"Okay," Aaron replied as he followed Frair to the tree line.

Roupert turned to Cassy. "Come; let us see if we can find some fresh meat. We will need our strength for tomorrow, and this will give us time to discuss our plan of attack."

***

The fire in the pit roared, as sparks danced in the night sky. Cassy was tired. She had eaten her fill of the roasted meat and was surprised how much she enjoyed it. In all of her life, Cassy never had thought she would enjoy hunting and preparing a meal over a roaring fire. This trip to the Kingdom of Walandra had opened her eyes to a new way of life, and she had to admit she liked it.

"Oh, man, I ate too much," Aaron groaned as he lay back on his blanket, rubbing his over-stuffed stomach.

"I was surprised one as small as you could eat so much of the roasted beast," Roupert chuckled.

"I couldn't help myself. It was so good. I wonder when we get home if Dad will take me hunting," Aaron smiled as he licked his lips.

"Well, I hope you have large beasts in your realm because you have a healthy appetite," Frair laughed as he rubbed his own over-filled stomach.

HOME. The word almost sounded foreign to Cassy's ears now. When she had first arrived in Walandra, it was always in the forefront of her thoughts, but now...

"Hey, what are you thinking, Sis?" Aaron noticed Cassy lost in her thoughts.

"Huh? Ah, nothing really, I'm just enjoying the beautiful evening after our grand feast." She hoped this answer would suffice.

"We owe our feast to Cassy," Roupert said with pride shining in his eyes.

Aaron sat up with a look of surprise on his face. "What? You mean Cassy killed the beast?"

Roupert laughed at the look of surprise on Aarons's face. "Yes, she stalked the beast, and when it turned its back on her to continue eating, she killed it with one strike of my sword."

Aaron's eyes were wide with excitement. "Oh, man, I wish I would have seen that. Cassy, you're a great hunter now!"

"Yes, I am impressed too," Frair's eyes beamed with excitement.

"I was only doing as Roupert instructed." While she appreciated the praise, it still caused her cheeks to glow a soft shade of red. Cassy had never imagined herself doing anything like that, but something was changing inside of her. She did not know what it was, but she had to admit she liked it.

"Well, forget about Dad teaching me to hunt. I want you to show me," Aaron said excitedly.

Cassy looked over at Aaron, "I don't think that would be a good idea. I'm sure our parents won't allow me to keep a sword in my room."

Aaron was about to protest then thought better of it. "You're right; it would freak them out to know you killed a beast with nothing but a sword. I think it's totally awesome."

Cassy understood the reason Roupert had wanted her to make the kill. He knew she would need to know the feel of the sword in her hand, as well as how it felt to take a life when she faced the Evil Queen Alona and her guards.

Cassy had never thought of herself as a warrior, but that was precisely what she was now. She would have to face dangers she had never dreamt of and somehow find the inner strength not only to conquer the Evil Queen but also to survive.

"Thank you, Aaron, for your faith in me. It means a lot." Cassy only hoped she could live up to the belief placed in her.

Realizing Cassy was in no mood for conversation, Aaron turned to Frair.

"I don't understand something. I thought dragons were supposed to be big and scary creatures."

Frair shook his head, unsure of what Aaron meant. "I do not understand your words. Why would you believe a dragon would be big and scary? I am the only one of my kind, so what gave you that idea?"

"I've read stories of great fire-breathing dragons, and..." Roupert cut him off before he could continue.

"It is late, and we need to rest. You may pursue this conversation once we defeat the Evil Queen," Roupert swallowed hard, hoping Frair would not challenge his command.

At seeing the determined look on Roupert's face, both Aaron and Frair decided it was best to leave this conversation for a later time.

"Yes, you are correct. We need our rest," Frair yawned as he lay back on a pile of soft grass. As he closed his eyes, his mind wandered back to what Aaron had said about stories of big fire-breathing dragons.

How is that possible? Roupert told me I am the only one of my kind, the words swirled around in his mind as he drifted off to sleep.

Chapter 14

The sun peeked over the tree line, casting its warm glow down on the sleeping group. Still feeling a slight chill in the air, Cassy pulled her blanket up tightly around her neck. "I don't want to wake up yet."

"Me either," Aaron groaned.

Roupert sat up, rubbing his eyes. "I know, but we must discuss our plans before leaving. Frair, will you please start the fire?"

Once he heard no response, Roupert turned to where Frair had made his bed the night before. "Frair, where are you?"

***

Panic gripped the group as they frantically searched for Frair.

"I don't understand, he was there when I fell asleep last night," Aaron cried.

Roupert felt a tightening in his chest. "Alona!"

Cassy felt her heart nearly stop beating with the fear Alona had somehow taken Frair. "Do you think she has him?"

"That is my fear. She must have learned of his existence. If she learns of his true identity…" Roupert felt his heart consumed with fear.

Aaron watched helplessly as Cassy and Roupert spoke. "I don't understand what you mean about his true identity, and why would the Evil Queen want Frair?"

Cassy and Roupert exchanged glances, unsure of what to say.

"Come on, Frair is our friend. If the Evil Queen took him, I want to know why," Aaron cried.

Roupert reached out and rested his hand on Aaron's shoulder. "I have not been entirely honest with Frair about his past."

Aaron narrowed his eyes, wondering what could be so terrible about Frair's past.

Roupert drew in a deep breath, trying to gather his thoughts before he spoke. "Frair is a member of the Royal Family. He is Prince Frair, the beloved son of King Ashlym and Queen Privlana."

Aaron stood dumbfounded, not moving or blinking.

"On the day Queen Alona took over the Kingdom, I was entrusted by the Lillients to take the egg of the unborn Prince far away from the Kingdom and to keep him safe. I was to watch over it until the day the Champion came to free the kingdom from Queen Alona."

Aaron was surprised to learn the truth of Frair. His heart was beating wildly in his chest as Roupert continued.

"On that day, the Lillients commanded I do not reveal to Frair his heritage, or that his mother still lives enslaved in the Great Dungeon deep under the castle. They feared he would seek revenge against the Evil Queen and fall victim to her power."

Aaron stared at Roupert; his eyes wide with fear. "But if the Evil Queen has Frair, it's up to us to save him. We promised to do this together."

Cassy could see the concern in Aaron's eyes, and she had to agree with his desire to save Frair from Alona. Unfortunately, she knew they could not charge the castle for the Queen surely had a trap ready for them. "What can we do, Roupert? We can't leave Frair in her clutches."

"We have a plan," a small voice came from behind them.

Roupert, Cassy, and Aaron turned to see Arianna, Syrea, and Brianna hovering in front of them with their little wings rapidly beating in the air.

Cassy stepped forward. "What is your plan?"

Syrea spoke first. "First, you must know the Queen sent two Demlins to lure Frair to the castle under false pretenses. Their names are David and Ralph, and they are two of the vilest Demlins from the Land of Shadows. They appeared to Frair cloaked in the image of another dragon, thus making Frair believe he was of their clan from a distant realm. They told him he was one of the chosen to serve the great Queen Alona, as dragons have done from the dawn of time."

Cassy looked at the three Lillients and could see the fear in their eyes.

Now Brianna flew forward to speak. "They came to him in his dreams last night and told him

Roupert had been lying to him about who he was. They said Roupert stole him from Queen Alona before his birth because he wanted to control the vast power Frair would have once he grew to maturity."

Roupert watched the Lillients as they explained what had happened to Frair, and he felt his blood burn with rage. Closing his eyes, he envisioned striking down Alona with his sword. This image, of course, brought a smile to his lips.

"I understand your desire for revenge, Roupert, but the Champion must be the one to conquer the Queen. She is the only one who can lift the curse and restore the Kingdom to its once great glory," Brianna's voice took on a grave tone.

"That's not fair to see my thoughts. Besides, they are only thoughts. I know what must happen to remove the curse and restore the Kingdom." Roupert did not appreciate Brianna invading his mind and seeing his innermost feelings.

Cassy watched the exchange between Roupert and the Lillient and wondered why she had warned him. Then again, knowing her own feelings, she was sure she knew.

Aaron walked up and tugged on Cassy's sleeve. "Who are they?"

Cassy laughed then turned to face the Lillients. "This is Syrea, Arianna, and Brianna. They call themselves Lillients, and they are the ones who were guarding Frair when the Evil Queen attacked and took control of the Kingdom. They are the ones who Queen Privlana sent to

Roupert to watch over Frair when he was still in his egg."

Aaron looked up at the three Lillients and smiled. He then bowed in reverence. "Hello, it's an honor to meet you."

"We are honored to meet you, Aaron, brother of Cassandra," Syrea returned the smile, as the three of them bowed.

"So, what are we supposed to do to save Frair? If he believes Roupert has betrayed him, he won't trust us," Cassy questioned.

"Yes, we all know the burning desire he has fought all these years." Roupert felt heartache for lying to Frair about who he was and that he was the lone dragon.

"We all know the need for dragons to be with others of their kind, but you know that was impossible. Had Queen Alona known of Frair, she would have just taken him sooner. You taught him well, so we must hold on to the faith he will remember the bond you two have shared and not surrender to the darkness and hate from Alona." Arianna commented with sorrow showing in her eyes.

"Okay, standing around talking won't save Frair. We need to go get him," Aaron said with determination in his voice.

"You are quite brave, young Aaron, but you must not go to the castle. It is not safe for you," Brianna held up her hand as Aaron began to protest.

"Brianna is correct. It will be a great battle, and one of your young age does not need to fight."

Syrea pointed toward Aaron at seeing the disappointment in his eyes.

"That's not fair. I want to…" Aaron suddenly closed his eyes, appearing to be in a trance.

Cassy turned toward Aaron. "What have you done to him?"

"He will sleep until you have conquered the Queen," Syrea said without emotion.

"What? You can't just leave him here," Cassy moved her hand in front of his face, with no response.

"My child, we will not leave him here unattended. We will take him to our realm, where he will be safe," Brianna assured her.

"Okay, but what happens if I don't win against the Queen? What will happen to Aaron then?"

"Do not think that way, Cassandra. You will be triumphant over the Evil Queen," Arianna assured her.

"Fine, I hope I am, but if I'm not, what will happen to Aaron?" Cassy was tired of not getting any answers to her questions.

The Lillients exchanged nervous glances, then they turned to face Cassy.

Brianna spoke up first. "If you should fail in your quest to destroy Queen Alona, Aaron will suffer your same fate."

The words hit Cassy like a sledgehammer. "How is that possible? Why can't you just return him home?"

"They won't be able to return him to your home realm because Alona will have the power of the King's blood in the Blood Key. Aaron will be trapped here and under her control with the rest of us," Roupert spoke up.

Cassy looked at Roupert then back to the Lillients, tears filling her eyes. "Is that true?"

The three Lillients merely nodded their heads, acknowledging his words were true.

Cassy felt as though someone had just kicked her in the gut. "No, that can't be true."

"I'm sorry, but it is. So, you must be successful," Roupert tried to conceal the fear churning inside on him.

Realizing there was nothing more to say, Cassy leaned forward and gently kissed Aaron on the forehead. "I love you, little brother. I promise to destroy the Evil Queen so we can return home."

***

"I can't believe he was dishonest with me my whole life," Frair moaned with tears streaming down his cheeks.

"He was a traitor to the Queen, and he did not want you to know the truth," David smirked with a devilish smile on his lips.

"Yes, he wanted to keep you in the dark about who you really are," Ralph taunted, feigning concern.

The two Demlins looked at each other and cackled joyously, assured they had convinced the young Prince of the lie ordered by Queen Alona.

"I'm glad you found me before I helped them destroy our Queen. When do I get to meet her?" Frair fought to control his emotions.

"Soon, our friend, soon."

Chapter 15

Queen Privlana paced the dungeon floor, dragging the chain secured around her ankle behind her.

"What have I done? How could I have allowed Alona to see my thoughts?"

She knew the answer to that dreaded question. She had allowed her excitement of finally seeing her son consume her mind.

Her heart ached at knowing Frair was at the mercy of Alona and her evil magic. The worry and pain surging through Privlana grew to be overwhelming. She whispered a silent prayer of protection for Frair at what she knew would come.

"My Queen," a small voice penetrated the agonizing thoughts consuming Privlana's mind.

"Yes...what?" Privlana turned toward the sound of the gentle voice.

Perched on a stone protruding from the dungeon wall sat Keira, the Milif.

"I have come in answer to your question," Keira smiled, trying to calm Privlana.

"My question, I don't understand what you mean," Privlana said with a heavy heart.

"My Queen, it was not your fault. Everything is happening, as it must be."

Queen Privlana wiped the tears from her eyes, unsure of the meaning of Keira's words. "How can Alona knowing of my son be good? She will kill him," emotions overwhelmed Privlana as she thought of Frair in the hands of Alona.

"Do not fear for the young Prince. While at first, he will believe Alona's lies, his heart will soon learn the truth. He is a Dragon of the Royal Clan, so the truth lies deep inside of him. He will come to accept the truth soon enough. Roupert raised him well and loved him as a son. Do not fear, my Queen, all will be as it is meant to be."

Privlana felt a warm sense of peace flow over her as she gazed upon Keira.

She had lived in fear for so many years it had grown difficult to feel hope. She looked at Keira, wiped the tears from her eyes, and squared her shoulders.

"What do you have planned, Keira?"

***

Once the Lillients had left with Aaron, Cassy turned to Roupert. "Okay, what do we do first?"

Roupert combed his hand through his hair, trying to decide the best course of action. He knew they could not just storm the castle, for Queen Alona had surely put her best guards around the perimeter and at the gates.

"I'm not quite sure, but we must be careful not to act carelessly, for I know she is prepared for our attack."

Cassy felt her knees grow weak at his words. "I thought you'd know how to get inside unseen. You were a guard there once, right?"

Roupert saw the concern in her eyes, and, to be honest, he felt the same fear consuming him. When he had realized Frair was gone, his heart nearly stopped beating in his chest. While he always knew he had a great affection for Frair, he never realized just how deeply those feelings went. Roupert closed his eyes as the memory of the day Frair came forth in life from the egg, and the joy his heartfelt the first time he looked into Frair's emerald green eyes. That was when he knew he would fight any enemy and lay down his life for the young Prince.

"Roupert, are you okay. Come on, we don't have time for daydreaming." Cassy reached up and tugged on his shirt sleeve, drawing him out of the memory.

"I'm sorry; I'm just so worried about Frair. I fear Alona will harm him should he challenge her."

Roupert's words made no sense to Cassy. "Why would Frair challenge Alona? He does not know who she is or what she did. I can't imagine her telling him she killed his father and enslaved his mother in the dungeon."

As Roupert listened to Cassy, he suddenly understood why the Blood Key had chosen her.

"I believe Alona will try to convince him she is on his side. Everything I've heard since I've been here is, she craves the Power of the Dragon. She tried to get it from the King, but Queen Privlana prevented that. So, her only chance now is to get it from the King's only living son: Frair."

Roupert stood in amazement at the brilliance of her words. *Of course, Alona would want to convince Frair she was on his side, and everything he knew was a lie.*

A smile appeared on Roupert's face. "You are correct. That is precisely what she would do. Cassy, you are brilliant!"

Roupert grabbed Cassy, pulled her close to him, and held her in a tight embrace. "Thank you. Thank you for restoring my faith in the Champion."

Cassy laughed as Roupert released her from his grasp. "Well, I'm glad I have your faith Now, let's figure out how we're going to get inside that castle without being caught."

They both stood in silence for several moments, unsure of what to do. Each knew it must be a perfect plan, but neither had the slightest idea of how to accomplish the feat.

Cassy shook her head and laughed. "I have nothing, how about you?"

Roupert shrugged his shoulders. "Neither do I, I do worry that the Queen will more than likely have extra guards posted around the castle."

"Come on, this is a magical realm. There has to be a way to get inside the castle unseen," Cassy reached up and touched the Blood Key absent-mindedly.

"Did you just say something," Cassy turned toward Roupert.

"No, I haven't said anything."

"I can get you into the castle without the Evil Queen knowing."

Cassy and Roupert exchanged surprised expressions.

"You didn't say that did you," Roupert said.

"No, and that wasn't you, was it?" Cassy's eyes were wide with fear.

"I said it," the voice grew louder.

"Who are you, and where are you?" Cassy struggled to see where the voice was coming from.

"I am here, sitting on the toadstool," the voice said in a firm tone.

Cassy and Roupert turned and looked at the small creature sitting on a toadstool not far from where they stood.

"What is that?" The words had escaped Cassy's mouth before she realized saying them.

"It's Bonert, he's an Elim," Roupert said with a hint of disgust in his voice.

Bonert jumped from the toadstool, then he began to grow until he stood nearly five-feet-tall.

"Hello Roupert, it's nice to see you again," Bonert said with a hint of sarcasm in his voice.

"Well, I can't say it's good to see you again. What brings you to this part of the Kingdom? I thought you were banished to the Northern Mountains after your last fiasco."

"Roupert, I was never banished. It was just strongly suggested I return to my people there," Bonert replied with a mischievous smile on his face.

"Call it whatever you want. I seem to remember you were lucky to escape with your life after what you did," Roupert grinned with a hint of joy at Bonert's trouble.

Seeing that he was getting nowhere with this line of conversation, Bonert decided it was time to change the subject.

"So, who is this lovely young lady you are traveling with, Roupert?" Bonert bowed his head toward Cassy.

Roupert suddenly felt an uneasy feeling come over him. "She is no one of your concern."

As Cassy listened to the two of them banter back and forth, she could not help but watch Bonert. He was a strange-looking creature with his hooked shaped nose and large, coal-black eyes. His hands were large for his frame with long thin fingers and sharp broken fingernails. He was quite disgusting to look at in his filthy clothes, and Cassy understood why Roupert was not pleased to see him.

Bonert turned and faced Cassy. "Is it true you worry about getting inside of Queen Alona's castle undetected? I could have sworn I heard you utter those words."

Roupert stepped forward, placing himself between her and Bonert. "You do not want help from this…this…"

"Now, now, my old friend, name-calling is so beneath us, is it not?" Bonert smiled.

Roupert glanced over at Cassy and saw a look of concern flash across her face. He knew he must control his emotions, so as not to give Bonert the upper hand.

"You are right. Name-calling is below us. On the contrary, warning her of your treacherous ways and how making a deal with you can only lead to ruin, is not off-limits," Roupert glared at Bonert, challenging him to respond.

Cassy had heard enough bickering. "Gentlemen, we don't have time for you two to argue over old disagreements. The Evil Queen has Frair, and should she be able to get his power, we are all screwed."

Bonert and Roupert looked at each other with a look of confusion on their faces.

"What does this word screwed mean?" Bonert asked while Roupert nodded his head in agreement.

Cassy exhaled with frustration. "When one is screwed, it means you have no hope. It means we will lose if Alona obtains Frair's powers."

Bonert paused a moment then he nodded his understanding. "Yes, should the Evil Queen obtain the Power of the Dragon from Frair, the entire Kingdom is screwed, as you say."

"Cassy, you do not need his help. You can use your own powers just as you did at the river." Roupert hoped this would change her mind.

Bonert smiled. "So, the stories are real? The Breast Plate and Blood Key do give the wearer magical powers."

"Stop listening to him. He will only use your trust against you," Roupert pleaded.

Cassy was at a loss for what to do. On the one hand, she wanted to heed Roupert's warning, but the chance that Bonert could help her conquer Queen Alona was too difficult to pass.

"Give me a moment, I need to think. I know we need to be careful, and I know if we make the wrong decision, we will lose. I do not intend to allow Alona to destroy Walandra, and I do not intend to let her kill Frair or Aaron either."

Bonert could see the conflicted emotions consuming Cassy, which pleased him greatly.

"I understand your concern, and I want you to know I only came to help you on this quest. Queen Alona is powerful and cunning, so you will need to catch her by surprise." He stepped forward and reached out, trying to touch the Blood Key.

Cassy stepped back, surprised by this bold attempt. "What are you doing?"

"I told you not to trust him. He only seeks the power of the Blood Key," Roupert said with hate and mistrust burning in his eyes.

Bonert pulled his hand back and put it behind his back. "I meant no harm. I only wanted to feel it, that's all."

Cassy looked at Bonert, not convinced he was completely honest with her. She wanted to walk away, but something kept making her want to believe his words.

"Okay, how can you help me to be triumphant over Queen Alona?" Cassy said with her eyes narrowed, showing her mistrust of him.

Seeing this would be his only opportunity to gain her complete trust, Bonert swallowed and took a moment to gather his thoughts before he spoke.

"You have a need to enter the castle without alerting the guards, correct?"

Cassy nodded her head.

"Then, once you are inside the castle, you have a need to get down to the Great Dungeon undetected, correct?" Bonert smiled when he saw her nod that she agreed again.

"If I understand the power given to you by the Blood Key, your abilities only last for as long as you need them, am I correct?"

Roupert stepped forward. "Don't answer any more of his questions. He will only use the information against you."

Cassy turned toward Roupert, letting him know she did not appreciate his constant interruptions. At seeing this, Bonert cleared his throat then continued.

"You need something that will make your powers more lasting. The last thing you need is to make it to the castle only to have your abilities stop working in front of the Queen's guards, or worse, in front of the Queen herself." Bonert stopped long enough to let his words sink into Cassy's mind.

"This all sounds good, but what can you do for her she can't already do herself?" Roupert fought the desire to grab Bonert by the throat and choke the life out of him.

"That's true, what can you do for me?" Cassy wanted to believe Bonert, but she still was not sure if she could.

"I can show you if you'd like. That is, of course, as long as Roupert doesn't mind," Bonert snarled in a dismissive tone.

Cassy glanced over at Roupert, "I don't see any problem with him showing us."

Roupert wanted to yell at the top of his lungs how it was a mistake to trust Bonert, but he decided to trust Cassy's judgment. "Fine, as you wish."

Bonert reached inside his pocket and pulled out a small pouch. Cassy watched as he poured what appeared to be dried flower blooms in the palm of his hand. He then held up his hand and smiled.

"These flowers grow in the meadows outside of my village. They contain unique magical properties when eaten by those who already have the power of magic within them."

Cassy leaned forward and looked at the dried flowers in his hand. "Okay, so just what do they do?"

Bonert looked up into Cassy's eyes, and he could see the strength hidden behind the fear shining in them. "All you need to do is eat one of the flowers whenever you want to be warned of impending danger. The flower will give you the gift of sight, so you will know when the Queen's guards are near."

Cassy glanced up at Roupert. "That would be helpful."

Roupert shook his head. He was not convinced of Bonert's honesty. "Cassy, I'm not sure…"

"I see my old friend, Roupert still does not trust my intentions to help you on your quest. That saddens my heart," Bonert feigned sorrow then was pleased to see a look of sadness appear on Cassy's face.

"Roupert, I believe Bonert actually wants to help us. He would have nothing to gain by misleading us," she smiled at Bonert.

Roupert knew there was no sense in arguing anymore. He would just have to watch carefully over Cassy and pray the power of the Blood Key would keep her safe.

"Roupert, did you hear what I said?" Cassy asked.

"Yes, I understand, even though I do not agree with your decision," he groaned.

Bonert smiled as he watched the discussion between Cassy and Roupert. *Excellent, I have planted the seed of discontent between them as instructed.*

"Okay, now the important question. What do you want for these?" Cassy asked.

Bonert looked up into her eyes then lowered them in a bow of reverence. "Normally, I would request much for a substance such as this. Yet, for you, I only require knowing my gift will help to free the Kingdom of Walandra from the clutches of the Evil Queen Alona." He poured the dried flowers back into the pouch, then he held it out to Cassy.

Cassy took the pouch from Bonert. When their hands briefly touched in the exchange, she had a strange feeling move through her, but once he pulled his hand away, the feeling vanished.

"Thank you, Bonert, for your help." She then opened the pouch and pulled out one of the dried blooms.

Roupert turned his head away, not wanting to watch her make this dreaded mistake to trust Bonert.

"Remember to have faith in the sacred Breast Plate and Blood Key, our young Champion," Bonert said with a twisted grin on his face.

Cassy reached out and took Roupert's hand in hers, as she put the bloom on her tongue and closed her eyes. She searched her mind for the best way to get safely into the castle when it came to her.

As Bonert watched the two figures transform, he began to laugh. "Safe travels, little girl, for the Queen awaits your arrival."

Chapter 16

"Oh, my head hurts," Cassy groaned as she tried to stand. "What happened, and where are we?"

"I don't know, but we are not in the castle," Roupert held out his hand to help Cassy to her feet.

"I don't understand what happened. After I had placed the flower on my tongue, I thought of us transporting to the dungeon where Alona is holding Queen Privlana."

Cassy rubbed her eyes, trying to clear her vision. "This doesn't look like a dungeon."

"It's not. I brought you here for your own protection," Keira said, as she appeared before Cassy.

Cassy shook her head, not understanding what Keira meant.

"Cassandra, you were warned not to trust everyone. You knew there were those who would do you harm should you give them a chance. Bonert was one of those who did not have your best interest at heart."

Cassy glanced at Roupert and saw the disappointment in his eyes.

"I told you not to trust him, but you wouldn't listen. Who knows what would have happened to you had Keira not acted?"

Cassy knew he was right. She had acted foolishly and nearly cost them their lives. "I'm sorry, I just thought…"

Keira drew closer to Cassy. "No, you did not think. You wanted to take the easy way and trust the wrong person. You have all the magic you need, so why do you continue to question yourself?"

Cassy hung her head in shame. Keira and Roupert were right. She had tried to take the easy way, and in the process, she had nearly handed herself and Roupert into the waiting hands of Queen Alona.

"You're right. I was a fool, and for that, I am truly sorry. Tell me then, what should I do? How can I use the Power of the Blood Key to get Roupert and me safely inside the castle?"

Keira glanced over at Roupert and smiled. "I believe our Champion is ready to fulfill her destiny now. Sit and listen."

In a flash of light, two stools appeared. Cassy and Roupert sat on them, each wondering what plan Keira had for them.

Keira's face took on a serious expression as she began to explain what they should do to conquer Queen Alona.

"Your first mistake was to think you could just pop into the dungeon and save Queen Privlana. Do you not think Queen Alona would have thought of that already?"

Cassy nodded her head as shame filled her heart.

"You must not think like a child. You are the chosen Champion, so you must think as such. Queen Alona has a spell cast to keep you out of the dungeon, thus, away from Queen Privlana. She knows once you are able to restore the sacred Breast Plate to Queen Privlana, the power of the Blood Key will belong to her. The only way you will ever get inside of the dungeon is to lift the spell preventing your entry into the dungeon."

Cassy lifted her face, her gaze meeting Keira's. "I don't understand how I can do that. How can I lift the spell? Do I have the power to do something like that?"

Keira shook her head as sadness filled her eyes. "You did. That is until Queen Alona sent the Demlins to lure Frair away with their lies."

Cassy thought for a moment, trying to understand Keira's words. "Are you saying with the power of the Blood Key and the powers Frair has from his Dragon's blood is how I would have lifted the spell over the dungeon? Oh, that's just great," Cassy moaned, realizing she had had everything she needed all along.

Roupert sat and listened carefully to everything Cassy, and Keira said.

Keira turned and looked at Roupert, sensing his question. "You want to know why I didn't tell Cassy all of this before, correct?"

"As a matter of fact, yes, I would love to know why you waited to tell her now," Roupert fought to control his anger and disappointment.

"I can only help. I cannot lead. She never asked the needed questions, so I could not offer any answers. I know it may seem strange, but that is how it works. I only pray I have not overstepped my bounds by bringing you here," Keira shrugged her shoulders and grinned sheepishly.

Cassy glanced around, trying to get a gauge of where they were.

"I seem to know this place," Roupert said, as he scanned the area.

"As you should, Sir Roupert. This is where you hid Abigail from the Evil Queen when she was the Champion." Keira smiled when she saw his eyes light up with the memory of Abigail.

"So, you really did know my great-grandmother? Aaron, my sister and I call her Queen Abigail, and we are her little Prince and Princesses," Cassy grinned at seeing his cheeks flush at the mention of Abigail's name.

"Yes, she was very special to me," he turned away, trying to hide his feelings for Abigail.

Realizing he was uncomfortable speaking of that time, Cassy decided it was best to work on the task ahead of them.

"So, tell me, Keira, how can we get safely inside of the castle without alerting the guards, and how do we find Frair?"

"Finding Frair will be quite easy, for once you find Queen Alona, you will find Frair. Yet, on the other hand, getting safely inside of the castle will be far more challenging." Keira knew these words were not the ones Cassy wanted to hear, but they were the truth.

"Oh, that's just great. First, you're telling me it will be nearly impossible to get inside the castle undetected by the guards. Then the only way I can break the spell that prevents me from entering the dungeon is to rescue Frair, but he will more than likely be with Queen Alona. Oh, yeah, that sounds like no problem at all," the words betrayed her lack of faith in herself.

Keira knew Cassy was worried, but the duties of the Champion were trying. "Yes, I do believe you understand everything correctly."

"Understand everything perfectly? You have got to be kidding me. The only thing I know is Roupert, and I are probably going to die at the hands of Queen Alona, and my brother will find himself trapped in this realm forever. Yep, that's about everything I was supposed to understand, right?" Cassy felt all hope for a successful ending evaporate from her being.

Keira understood Cassy's fear, but she knew if she were to surrender now, all was lost for the subjects of Walandra.

"Do not let this fear consume you, Cassandra. You are stronger than you realize. The sacred Breast Plate and Blood Key chose you for that strength, so now you need to believe in it as well."

Cassy glanced over to Roupert, who nodded his encouragement. "She's right, you know. It chose you because it was in you to handle this task. I have faith in you. Now you only need to have confidence in yourself."

Cassy shook her head, not wanting to accept their words. "I'm just a kid. A few days ago, the only thing I was worried about was if I'd make the school soccer team. I'm no warrior. I don't know how to fight evil Queens or her palace guards. I just want to go home and be a teenager again."

Keira reached up and placed her tiny hand on Cassy's cheek. "I understand your fears, and you would be wise to hold on to them some, but you are much more than a teenager who only wants to play ball in school. You have greatness buried deep within you. It will not only help you defeat Queen Alona but will also guide you in your life once you return home to your realm. Do not question your abilities, Cassandra. For you have an exciting life ahead of you."

Cassy wanted to believe Keira's words, but her doubts prevented her from fully accepting them. "Okay, I'll do my best, but I only hope my best is good enough."

***

Queen Privlana sat on a filthy mat in the corner of the dungeon, searching her mind for what she could do to save Frair. She knew the Lillients would watch over him to the best of their ability, but if Alona had found a way around their protection, all hope was lost.

"How could I have allowed her to see into my memories?"

She knew the answer to her question. In her excitement to be with her son, she had let down her guard.

"Oh, Ashlym, my beloved, how much longer must I wait? My spirit grows weak, trapped in this form. How I long for my Dragon's heart beating in my chest again as I fly through the sky with you by my side. To have spent all these years trapped in this dark and dreary place, away from everyone I love. It has nearly drained my will to live." She covered her eyes and wept bitterly.

"Your Majesty, do not cry; for the Champion comes to free you from your bondage," Syrea, of the Lillients, whispered in Privlana's ear.

Privlana jumped back, startled by the soft voice. "How is it possible? How is it you are able to get past Alona's spell?"

Syrea laughed softly, "Her magic has no power over the magic of the Lillients. Light Magic always has power over Dark Magic."

Privlana tipped her head to the side, unsure if she understood the statement. "I don't understand. If that is the case, why is my magic powerless against her? The magic of the Dragon has always been that of Light."

"That is true, My Queen; however, when Alona cast the curse over your family, she bound your powers. You will not have your powers again until the day the curse is broken." Syrea felt Privlana's pain and wished she could end her sorrow.

Privlana lowered her face, ashamed to look at Syrea. "I owe you so much. You came to me when I needed you most. You made sure my son had made it safely out of the castle before Alona was able to find him. Now I have another thing to ask of you."

Syrea looked deeply into Privlana's eyes, seeing the fear behind the tears. "My Queen, I know your concern for Frair. I know you worry the Champion will fail like the one before. I am here to tell you not to give up hope. This Champion is much stronger than Abigail was. She has a keen wit, is willing to face her adversary, and has much love in her heart for those who are important to her. Those are excellent qualities for a Champion," Syrea smiled when she noticed Privlana seem to relax.

"I hope you are correct, for I do not know how much longer I can last chained in this dungeon," Privlana groaned.

"Please know you are never alone. I am aware Keira, the Milif, has been to see you. Her powers are strong. She will watch over the Champion and keep her safe." Syrea wiped a stray tear from Privlana's cheek.

Privlana lifted her head and gazed into Syrea's eyes. "This Champion, may I ask her name?"

Syrea beamed with excitement. "Her name is quite beautiful, it is Cassandra."

"Cassandra, yes, that is lovely. I look forward to meeting our Champion, Cassandra," Queen Privlana smiled.

Privlana sat silently for a few moments, trying to decide how to ask the question to answer her greatest fear.

"What is on your mind, my Queen?"

Privlana wanted to know of Frair, but she was too afraid to ask.

She knew not knowing would torment her soul, so Privlana looked at Syrea and blurted out the words without thinking.

"Should Alona find Frair, do you believe she would do him harm?"

Syrea did not respond immediately. She merely gazed into Privlana's tear-filled eyes. "I know Alona wants to have control of the Blood Key and all the power it holds. I also know she can use Frair and his powers to aid her in obtaining the Blood Key from the Champion."

"How do we stop that from happening?" Privlana asked.

"That my Queen is the greatest question of all."

Chapter 17

Several minutes had passed since Keira vanished, leaving Cassy and Roupert still unsure of what they should do. They both just stood in place, neither of them speaking until Cassy decided to break the silence.

"Why did you hide my great-grandmother here? What happened when she came here?"

Roupert had dreaded this moment. He had fought to bury his feelings for Abigail, but now he knew he would have to face them again. He closed his eyes for a moment, as the memories of his time with Abigail flooded into the forefront of his mind.

~~~

Lightning filled the sky on the day Abigail appeared in the Kingdom of Walandra. Roupert was returning from a hunt when he came across the frightened young woman, sitting under a tree along the path to his hut and crying with her hands covering her face.

"Are you okay?" he asked, trying not to startle her.

The young woman looked up at Roupert and nodded her head.

"I do not remember seeing you in this part of the forest before. Are you lost?" Roupert could see the confusion in her eyes, and he feared she was in some sort of danger.

The young woman nodded her head again.

Realizing he was not getting anywhere, Roupert decided to try something else.

"My name is Roupert. What is your name?" He held his breath and waited for her response.

She hesitated before answering, gazing solemnly at him. She breathed in deeply then said, "My name is Abigail; it's nice to meet you, Roupert."

As Abigail began to stand, Roupert offered his hand. "Here, let me help you."

"Thank you, that is very kind," Abigail blushed.

Once she had stood, Roupert stepped back, taken by surprise by what he saw. He lifted his hand and pointed at Abigail. "It's you," the words escaped his mouth.

Taken aback by the strange statement, Abigail began to cry again. "What is going on here? I was in my grandfather's library looking at one of his old books, and the next thing I know is I'm in this strange place and wearing this!" She pointed to the breastplate with the red gemstone in the center of it.

"You were chosen. What you are wearing is the sacred Breast Plate and Blood Key. It has chosen you to be the Champion." Roupert bowed his head in reverence.

Abigail glanced down at the breastplate then back up at Roupert. "This makes no sense. This was the stone in my grandfather's book. What's going on?"

Lightning flashed across the sky as thunder crashed in the distance. Soon the sky grew dark as the clouds released rain on the ground.

"Quick, we need to get to shelter before the storm becomes worse," Roupert offered his hand to Abigail with urgency in his voice.

She hesitated a moment, but when the lightning filled the sky again, she took his offered hand.

"Where are you taking me?" she said breathlessly as they quickly followed the path with the rain pelting down on them.

"To my hut, you will be safe there," Roupert quickened his pace much to Abigail's dismay.

By the time they reached the hut, both were thoroughly soaked from the rain. Roupert ran to the hut tucked among the trees, opened the door, and waited for Abigail to enter before he joined her inside.

"You look chilled. Let me start the fire," Roupert quickly walked over to the fire pit in the center of the hut and stoked the embers left from that morning, causing them to flare up. He then carefully placed a stick of dry wood on the small fire, along with a few twigs to help the fire burst into flames and begin to heat the room.

"As a matter of fact, I am a bit cold," she blushed when she saw the nervous expression on Roupert's face. "Maybe if I sit by the fire for a bit, I'll feel better."

"Yes, that's a good idea. Let the fire dry your clothes." For some reason, Roupert found it challenging to look at Abigail. He had spoken to several a young maiden in his life, but there was something different about her. He quickly brushed the dust from one of the wooden chairs sitting by the table and pulled it over by the fire.

"Please, sit, and warm yourself by the fire," Roupert muttered quietly while averting her gaze.

Abigail sat on the offered chair then leaned forward, enjoying the warmth of the flames on her hands. "Thank you for bringing me here. I would hate to think of being outside with the storm coming."

As their gazes met, Roupert felt his heart quicken in his chest. He turned his head and then grabbed another piece of wood and added it to the fire.

"This should warm you in no time. I will make us some root tea," he whispered nervously. He walked over to the shelf next to the table and grabbed a small jar, and then set it on the table.

"Root tea? I've never had root tea," Abigail smiled, as their gazes met again.

Realizing he was transfixed on her, Roupert turned his head and reached for the kettle, "I need to get some water. I'll return in a moment."

He picked up the kettle and rushed toward the door, glad to put some distance between him and the beautiful young maiden with the hypnotic eyes.

Once he was outside and had closed the door behind him, he leaned against the wall and exhaled a strained breath.

"What is wrong with me? Why do I feel so drawn to her?"

He shook his head then laughed at his foolishness. "You cannot have feelings for her; she is the Champion, chosen by the sacred Breast Place and Blood Key."

Just saying those words made pain fill his heart, for he knew what was ahead for the stunning beauty sitting beside the fire inside his hut.

He dipped the kettle into the rain barrel. He then turned and opened the door. He paused a moment before stepping inside with the hope he could control the strange emotions surging up from deep inside of his soul.

"I'm glad you're back. I was beginning to get lonely," Abigail teased playfully, hoping to ease the tension between them.

Roupert hung the kettle over the fire, trying to avoid her beautiful eyes. "The tea will be ready in a few minutes. Are you hungry?"

"No, not just yet; please sit, I have so many questions," Abigail pleaded.

Roupert felt his heart stop in his chest. "Ah, okay." He swallowed as he brought another chair over by the fire, keeping his distance from Abigail.

"Please come closer. I promise not to bite. I have lived with my Grandfather for most of my life, so I'm at ease speaking with men," Abigail laughed softly at seeing the shocked expression on his face.

"Besides, I have a feeling you are too much of a gentleman for me to fear."

Realizing he had no choice, Roupert pulled his chair closer to Abigail.

"There that's better, isn't it? You saved me from the storm, so there is no need for us to feel uncomfortable with each other." Abigail sensed kindness in this man who opened his home to her, and she found herself drawn to him.

Roupert glanced up at her and found himself lost in her beautiful eyes again. He had never felt this way before, and he wondered why he did now. "You were raised by your Grandfather, what happened to your parents?"

Abigail's eyes filled with tears as she told him of her parents and the tragic way they had died.

"Where is this? I know I'm not in Maine anymore," Abigail said with a hint of confusion in her voice.

"Maine, no, I do not know of that place. You are in the Kingdom of Walandra."

Abigail was at a loss for words. "I don't understand. How did I get here?"

Roupert reached out and gently touched the stone attached to the breastplate covering her chest. "The Blood Key brought you here."

"But that makes no sense. How can a red stone do that? It was on an old worn-out book my grandfather brought home from a faraway land. This is all insane," Abigail covered her face with her hands as frustration consumed her entire being.

Roupert felt troubled for Abigail. He knew she was scared, as anyone who was suddenly transported to a strange land away from everything they knew would be. Nonetheless, the Blood Key chose her as the Champion, and until she fulfilled her destiny, she would not return to her home.

He reached out and took her hand in his, trying to console her fears. Their gazes met again, and the same feeling overcame him, making him pull his hand away.

"I'm sorry… The water is warm," he jumped up and carried the kettle to the table to prepare the tea.

Abigail watched Roupert as he poured the hot water into the mugs, and then stirred in an amber-colored substance into the tea.

"I hope you do not mind, but I added some sweet sap to the tea," Roupert said nervously as he carried the mugs with him to where they were sitting by the fire.

"No, not at all; I like my tea sweet." Abigail took the offered mug, "Thank you."

Roupert nodded as he returned to his chair, not saying a word.

Several tense-filled moments passed as both struggled with what to say. It was Abigail, who finally broke the silence.

"Roupert, why did you call me the Champion? What did you mean by that?"

Roupert gazed upon the beautiful young maiden and wondered how he could tell her the truth. She seemed to be such a delicate being, not one to challenge the Evil Queen Alona. He prepared himself to tell her when a sense of panic overtook him.

"The fire grows weak. I'll go get some more wood," he quickly jumped to his feet and headed for the door.

Before Abigail could protest, Roupert had vanished through the door, closing it behind him.

"My, that was strange," she thought aloud.

Unsure of how long he would be gone, Abigail decided to use this time to explore the hut. "This shouldn't take long."

Abigail was amazed at how organized he had the small hut, as everything seemed to be in its proper place. She noticed the shelves with jars and pouches, as well as plates, bowls, and mugs. She walked over to the table and ran her hand along the top, feeling the smoothness of the wood.

"Very nice," she said as she turned to walk back to her chair by the fire.

"Oh, what was that?" She stopped and looked down at the object she had just kicked with her foot.

"Oh my, what is this?" Abigail gasped as she looked into the basket on the floor tucked under the table.

Abigail had never seen such a thing. Nestled in the basket on a bed of straw was a large golden egg. She reached out to touch the egg when…

"Stop, do not touch that!" a voice shouted, startling Abigail.

She quickly pulled her hand away. She then ran back to her chair and sat with her hands folded in her lap. "I'm sorry, I meant no harm," she cried, looking around for who had scolded her.

At that moment, Roupert came through the door and saw Abigail crying.

"What happened here?" He looked around the room.

"She nearly touched the Royal Egg," the voice said.

Roupert looked at Abigail and saw the fear in her eyes.

"I'm sorry, I meant no harm. It's just I've never seen anything like that before. So that's what it is; A Royal Egg? How interesting." Abigail glanced around the hut, trying to find the source of the strange voice.

"Come out, Brianna, and introduce yourself," Roupert said, trying not to laugh. "You nearly scared Abigail to death."

"I would not have scared her, had she not tried to touch the Royal Egg," Brianna said defensively.

"Well, I do not believe the Champion would come all this way to harm the Prince, do you?" Roupert said playfully.

Abigail gasped as the small creature with delicate wings flew towards her from the shadows, and she marveled how beautiful it was.

"What do you mean, the Champion? This is not..." Brianna placed her hand over her heart then began to cry with joy. "It is you. Please forgive me; I did not see the sacred Breast Place and Blood Key. I cannot begin to tell you how excited I am you are here. My name is Brianna of the Lillients. We are guardians of the Royal Eggs."

"It's nice to meet you, Brianna. My name is Abigail. None of this makes any sense to me, but I'm sure you and Roupert will explain it all to me in due time."

"Yes, dear Abigail. You are very special, and it is an honor to be at your service. I have a feeling the Blood Key has chosen well," Brianna bowed her head.

Abigail placed her hand on the Blood Key and felt a strange vibration and warmth go into her hand then through her entire being. "Oh my," she said with surprise.

"This is truly a joyous day, Roupert. It is one that we have awaited for many years. My sisters must know," Brianna closed her eyes when suddenly, two other Lillients appeared.

"See, my sisters; the Champion is here," Brianna said excitedly.

Brianna turned to the two Lillients and said, "This is Syrea and Arianna."

Syrea and Arianna bowed their heads then looked at Abigail with smiles on their faces.

"She is quite lovely," Syrea observed as the others nodded their heads in agreement.

"Do you not think she is lovely, Roupert?" Syrea said with a playful smile on her face.

"Ah, yes, she is," his cheeks grew warm and flushed as he realized what he had said.

"Stop teasing him. Can you not see he is taken with her?" Arianna chided Syrea then winked at Abigail.

Hoping to end this line of discussion, Roupert walked over and put some more wood on the fire.

"May I ask a question?" Abigail addressed the Lillients.

"Of course, what do you want to know?" Syrea answered.

"Why does Roupert have the egg here? If it's a Royal Egg, why isn't it in a castle instead of sitting in a basket here in this simple hut?" She hoped she had not offended him.

"That is why you are here, dear child," Arianna answered with compassion shining in her eyes.

Abigail sat transfixed as the Lillients told her the tale of how Alona tricked King Ashlym and Queen Privlana, taking control of the Kingdom of Walandra. As they shared the story, Abigail rested her hand on the Blood Key, feeling the strange vibration moving through her. Once the Lillients had completed the tale, Abigail understood her destiny, and through the power of the Blood Key, she had a clear understanding of how to accomplish it.

"May I see the Royal Egg again?" Abigail asked in a firm voice.

The Lillients exchanged concerned looks then nodded.

Abigail stood and walked over to the basket, then carefully set it on the table. A sudden rush of emotions overtook her as she gazed down at the Golden Egg nestled safely in the straw.

"He's lonely," Abigail said flatly.

"He's what?" Roupert asked both surprised and unsure if he had heard her correctly.

Abigail turned toward Roupert. "I said; he's lonely. Prince Frair feels alone. He told me," she reached out and gently touched the egg.

"I don't understand. Why didn't he let me know?" Roupert walked over to the basket.

"It's because she wears the Blood Key," Syrea explained as the other Lillients nodded their heads in agreement.

"Yes, the King's blood calls out to his son," Brianna said with tears of joy forming in the corners of her eyes.

"What else does he tell you?" Arianna said excitedly.

With her hand resting on the egg, Abigail closed her eyes and opened her mind to the thoughts of the young Prince.

"He says he has waited long to come forth into the world, and he is thankful to Roupert for caring for him all these long years. He says the spirit of his father has come to him and told him of a Champion that would restore the Kingdom and free its people from the reign of the Evil Queen, but he was to stay inside the egg until the Champion made themselves known. He wants you to know this knowledge has given him peace all these long years."

Roupert reached out and touched the egg as tears streamed down his cheeks. "I'm sorry; I did not know you were lonely all this time. I wish I would have known for so was I."

Abigail took Roupert's hand in hers, and suddenly he could hear the young Prince's thoughts. His eyes opened wide with surprise as he laughed at the thoughts of the Prince filling his mind.

After several moments, he released her hand and stepped away from the basket with tears of joy, wetting his cheeks.

Abigail turned to face Roupert. Her face was aglow with joy. "He loves you, you know, and he's thankful for everything you've done to keep him safe all these years."

Overtaken with joy, Roupert took Abigail in his arms and held her tightly. "Thank you; thank you for allowing me to know he's alright. I have worried all these years something was wrong since he had remained in the egg."

Abigail glanced at the Lillients and realized they were also crying. "Oh my, we are quite a bunch tonight, aren't we?"

"He likes you as well, Abigail and Prince Frair think you are beautiful. He does say he is surprised the Champion would be so young," Roupert saw a look of concern appear on Abigail's face.

Abigail felt everyone looking at her, and honestly, she had wondered the same thing. "I don't know why it would choose me. I'm a seventeen-year-old girl from Maine. I have lived most of my life on an island in a huge mansion, reading books and playing chess with my grandfather whenever he would return from his travels. I wish I knew the answer to his question, but I don't."

"It does not matter why it chose you, Abigail. All that matters is you are here now," the words left Roupert's mouth before he realized what he had said.

"See, it is true, he is taken with her," Arianna teased, as joyous laughter filled the room.

Chapter 18

Cassy sat mesmerized by the tale of how her great-grandmother Abigail had come to be the Champion. She looked over at Roupert and could see the sadness in his eyes as he spoke of Abigail and wondered if she had returned his feelings.

"I don't understand something. If Frair knew of his father and mother while he was still in the egg, why doesn't he know any of that now?"

"You see, when Queen Privlana cast her protection spell over the Dragon clan, she also cast a spell that would prevent Frair from remembering once he came forth from the egg."

Cassy's eyes lit up with excitement. "You were forbidden to tell him, weren't you?"

"Yes, I was forbidden to tell him the truth, and all memory of his true identity was stricken from the minds of the subjects of the Kingdom until Alona's curse is lifted." Roupert looked at her with sadness, clearly showing on his face.

Cassy shook her head, amazed at how everything fell into place. "So, tell me what happened? Why wasn't Abigail able to lift the curse and restore the Kingdom?"

Roupert hung his head with tears filling his eyes. "We were able to get Abigail into the dungeon and were about to reunite the sacred Breast Plate with Queen Privlana, but something happened that none of us expected," his voice cracked as his emotions overwhelmed him.

Cassy held her breath, waiting for him to continue.

"I don't know how it happened, but Alona had somehow set a trap for us. Once Abigail was only mere feet away from Queen Privlana, a powerful force wrapped around Abigail and held her in place. I tried to free her, but I was unsuccessful. I could see the fear in Abigail's eyes as the force darkened and began to crush her."

Cassy's eyes were wide with fear, as Roupert told the tale, and she wondered if she would meet the same fate.

"Abigail cried out for me to save her, but I couldn't move, for my feet were held fast to the floor by some magical power. Alona laughed a wicked laugh and slowly walked toward Abigail with her hands outstretched. It was then when Queen Privlana cried out for the power of the Blood Key to save Abigail. Just as Alona was about to rip the Blood Key from the Breast Plate on Abigail's chest, she vanished, and then I awoke in my hut."

Cassy leaned back, holding her hand over the Blood Key. "Wow; that was too close."

Roupert nodded his head while he wiped tears from his eyes. "I had promised to protect Abigail, but I failed."

"You can't blame yourself for what happened. Someone must have alerted Alona, giving her the opportunity to set a trap. You were lucky, as it could have ended much worse for the two of you."

Roupert looked up at Cassy and again saw Abigail in her eyes. "May I ask you a question?"

"Certainly, anything," Cassy reached over and gently touched his hand.

Roupert swallowed then lifted his eyes, meeting hers. "Has she lived a happy life?"

Cassy saw the sadness in his eyes, and then it came to her. "You're in love with her, aren't you?"

Roupert turned away, not wanting to meet her gaze. "I have no right to speak of such feelings."

"You do love her. I can tell by the way you speak of her."

Roupert turned and looked Cassy directly in the eyes. She could see the torment hiding behind the tears, and her heart filled with sadness.

"Yes, I've loved her from the first moment we met."

Cassy had no idea how to respond to such a confession of undying love. She sat a moment trying to gather her thoughts, but for the life of her, the proper words seemed to evade her.

"I'm sorry; I should not have asked such a question. I just thought…" Roupert fought to control his feelings.

"No, don't feel that way. You have every right to know. I haven't been around my great-grandmother much, but from what I understand, she has had a life mixed with great happiness and great sorrow. She really is a special lady, and I'm so glad we got to go visit her while our parents went on their vacation. She does seem happy for the most part."

"You said you have a sister. Please tell me of her," Roupert felt his emotions beginning to calm at knowing Abigail was happy.

Cassy looked at Roupert, rolled her eyes then laughed. "Melissa is my twin sister, and other than the fact we look exactly alike, any similarities end there. While I enjoy sports and hanging out with my friends, she's all into clothes and going to the mall with her small circle of fashion divas."

"I do not understand what a fashion diva is," Roupert grinned after Cassy rolled her eyes again.

"It's where a girl will only wear clothes that are designer and in style. Heck, you put me in a pair of old blue jeans and an over-sized tee shirt, and I'm a happy girl," Cassy laughed so hard that her sides began to hurt.

Roupert could not help but laugh as well. "Your sister sounds like some of the maidens in the castle village. I think that is why you and I get along so well. We are both simple souls," he winked playfully.

Cassy was glad to see a smile on his face, and she was pleased to learn what happened when her great-grandmother had faced Alona.

"Cassy, it grows late, and I fear we should wait until tomorrow before we enter the castle. We will be safe here, and that way, we can discuss what we need to do to reunite the Blood Key and Breast Plate with Queen Privlana."

Cassy looked around the small clearing and wondered if they were actually safe. She trusted

Roupert, but she also had a nagging feeling tugging at her.

"Okay, if you feel that's best. I am a bit tired," she yawned then rubbed her eyes.

"Good. Let us eat, then we will discuss our plans for tomorrow." Roupert opened his pack and pulled out the pouch with dried meat and the one with seeds and nuts.

"It's not a fancy meal, but it will keep us strong." He reached inside one of the pouches and pulled out a strip of dried meat then handed it to Cassy.

"Thank you." She took the offering and took a big bite. "This stuff really is good."

Roupert watched as she struggled to chew the tough meat.

"Here, take a drink of water to help wash it down," he chuckled as he handed her a pouch with water.

Cassy quickly took a drink of the water, with it dribbling down her chin. "Thanks, it seems to suck up all the moisture in your mouth."

Roupert took a piece out of the pouch for himself, and then he took a bite. "Yes, it does, but it tastes good," he winked as she took another bite.

***

Frair had waited for hours to meet Queen Alona, and he was beginning to wonder if he had made a mistake by leaving Roupert.

"How much longer do I have to wait?" he asked David, the Demlin sitting across from him in the dimly lit room.

"I do not know. Ralph has gone to report to our Queen, so once he returns, we will know more."

Frair looked around the room, trying to get a better idea of where he was. "Why do you keep it so dark in here? Do you not have a torch or candle?"

"We keep the room dark because that is how it is in our realm. You would know this had Roupert not lied to you all these years," David smirked devilishly.

"Oh, I'm sorry." Frair hoped David was not angry with him. He did not understand how he could come from such a dark realm as he never had liked the dark.

Frair shifted around, trying to find a more comfortable position. "I'm hungry, when do we get to eat?"

David glared at Frair. "You will eat when the Queen says you may eat and not a moment before."

Frair was about to protest when the large door to the room opened wide.

"The Queen is busy and cannot see you now. You will have to wait until later," Ralph, the other Demlin announced.

"What, I still have to wait? I do not think I want to be here any longer. I want to go home," Frair fought back the tears forming in the corners of his eyes.

"What did you say? You say you want to go back home. No, you foolish child, this is your home now. You are to serve Queen Alona and do her bidding. You have forgotten your duty, and it is not living with the traitor Roupert. You are a Dragon, and you must serve the Queen. Should Roupert come to the castle searching for you, you are to strike him dead. Do you understand?" Ralph's eyes glowed red with anger.

Frair suddenly had a sickening feeling overcome him, and he realized David and Ralph must surely have lied to him about Roupert and his past.

"I will not kill Roupert. He is my friend," Frair said defiantly.

David stepped forward and looked deeply into Frair's eyes. "Oh, but you are wrong. You will be the cause of his death, as his love for you will blind him to our plans. He will come here of his own will, and he will sacrifice himself to save you."

"No, no, he is the bravest and smartest man I know, and you will never deceive him," Frair cried out.

David's eyes shone brightly with anticipation. "Brother, tomorrow will be a glorious day. Queen Alona will finally have the power of the Blood Key, and she will vanquish Queen Privlana to the Land of the Shadows for all eternity. As for Roupert, he will meet his death at the hands of his beloved Frair. Yes, tomorrow will truly be a glorious day."

Frair stood, with rage overtaking his body. "I will go and warn him of your treachery."

Frair closed his eyes, trying to block out the glares of Ralph and David. Then he pulled back his shoulders to release his wings and was surprised when nothing happened.

"What is wrong? Why won't they open?" Frair cried as he struggled to spread his wings.

Ralph stepped forward, laughing. "You silly child, you do not believe we would allow you to just fly away, do you?"

Frair fought back the tears as he tried again to open his wings.

"Do not hurt yourself, as you are not going anywhere. We have cast a spell that prevents you from leaving this room. You can try to fly, walk to the door or even attempt to climb out of the small window above you, but you will not achieve freedom from this room." Ralph pointed toward the small window up high on the wall.

"You see, we have an important task for you to perform, so you will remain here until you fulfill it," David laughed when he saw the frightened look appear on Frair's face.

"I don't understand why you would do this. I thought we were brother Dragons," Frair dropped to the floor, with all hope of escape sucked out of him.

David and Ralph howled with laughter.

"You really are a fool," Ralph taunted with his eyes glowing a fiery red.

"I do believe we need to show Frair what we truly are," David hissed with a look of complete joy burning on his face.

Frair looked back and forth between the two Demlins, unsure of what they meant. He was about to speak again when they both transformed from dragon forms into something hideous and frightening.

Frair quickly moved away from them, covering his mouth with both surprise and fear. "What are you? You are not dragons."

David stretched his long, slender, snake-like body as he towered over Frair. "No, we are not. We are Demlins from the Land of Shadows."

Ralph stretched his long slender body, as well. He then leaned over Frair, glaring down at him, as though ready to strike. "Do you have any idea how horrible it has been for us to be in your sickening form? Oh, my back is so stiff; I can barely move. Just the thought of being stuck as a dragon for much longer made me ill."

"I, I don't understand. I have been a fool. I trusted you, and you have betrayed me," Frair cried, realizing what must surely lie ahead for him.

"We may have betrayed you, but you have betrayed not only Roupert but the Champion. You will lead her into the trap which will allow Queen Alona to take possession of the Blood Key, gaining its great power," David chuckled at the look of fear on Frair's face transform into one of panic.

"I don't understand. Why is the Blood Key so important?" Frair tried to control the fear building inside of him.

Ralph looked at David and smiled. "Do you think we should tell him, brother?"

David glanced down at Frair and laughed softly, "I do not see where it would do any harm.

He can do nothing to stop what will happen tomorrow; Queen Alona has seen to that."

Ralph rubbed his hands together and let out a deep chuckle. "You are no ordinary Dragon, Frair. You see, you are the Royal Prince of Walandra, the only son of the great King Ashlym and Queen Privlana."

He waited a moment for this surprising information to sink into Frair's mind.

"What? That is impossible. I am the only one of my kind in the Kingdom," Frair felt his body quiver at this unexpected news.

"That is the lie Roupert told you. You see, your mother did not want you after your father died, so she sent you away with Roupert to live in the forest. Then she took her own life once the guilt of killing the King consumed her," David said with a complete look of satisfaction on his face.

"No, that cannot be true. How did my father die?" Frair's heart was consumed with sorrow.

"It was your mother's doing. She killed him," Ralph said gleefully.

"NO, NO, tell me no more," Frair held his hands over his ears, trying to block out the painful words.

Both David and Ralph laughed aloud at the pain consuming Frair at learning the truth about his identity. Frair rocked from side-to-side, crying until he was sure he would die. Everything he had believed in his life was a lie. Frair had always thought himself a mere creature of the forest, living happily with Roupert. Now he has learned he is a Prince, and that parents were part of some evil plan.

To learn his father had died because of his mother, and then learn she cast him away was more than he could handle. Frair closed his eyes in the attempt to block out the pain, but the devilish taunts of David and Ralph filled his senses.

"Come, Ralph, it grows late, and I wish to enjoy the feast awaiting us in the Great Hall," David sneered with a demonic gleam in his eyes.

"Yes. It's a shame Frair will not be joining us," Ralph gloated with feigned sadness.

"Please let me go. Let me return to my life in the forest. I promise that I will never come back. Queen Alona will never have to worry about me," Frair pleaded.

David and Ralph exchanged devious smiles and left the room without saying another word.

Once the door had slammed shut, Frair felt his heart lose all desire to live. How could this be happening? How could he have lived his entire life and not known the truth? He leaned his back against the cold stone wall and wondered what he could do to stop Queen Alona. He had nearly given up all hope when he heard a soft voice whispering in his mind.

"Frair, it is I; your mother."

Frair lifted his head and frantically looked toward the door. "Mother, where are you?"

"I am in the dungeon where Alona has kept me in bondage for all these years."

Frair looked around the room, convinced he had lost his mind. "No, that is not possible. You are dead."

"No, Frair; that is another lie. I have been here since Alona killed your father and trapped me in my human form. She tried to destroy our clan, but she was not successful. You see, evil will never win over good."

Frair shook his head, trying to understand her words. "But she has won, Mother, and now she plans to use me to complete her evil plan. How can I stop her? I do not want my friends to die."

"Son, you must not surrender to defeat. The Champion will face much adversity when she arrives at the castle. She will be tested, so you need to remain firm and believe in the power of the Blood Key."

"Mother, what gives the Blood Key its power. Why does Alona crave its power so much?"

Frair waited for an answer, but none came. "Mother, are you still there?"

"Yes, my son. I created The Blood Key from the powerful Blood Stone, which has great magical powers. Alona stole the Blood Stone from the Guardians and planned to increase its power by infusing it with the blood of the most magical of all creatures in our realm."

"I don't understand, Mother. Whose blood did she need?"

Privlana did not want to tell Frair, but she knew he deserved to know the truth. "The blood she needed was that of King Ashlym, the King of the Dragons and your father."

Wails of pain burst forth from Frair, filling the small room. He closed his eyes, forcing the anger to stay deep inside him for fear it would consume his soul. Alona had destroyed his family, and now she intended to destroy those he cared for most.

"Mother, what can I do to stop her? How can I prevent her from fulfilling her evil plan?"

"I'm not sure, my son. I do know you must fight against anything she may try to force you to do. She has great power and can bend your will to suit her needs. Therefore, you must not allow her to use you in that manner. I wish I could help you more, but I cannot."

Frair reached up and wiped the tears from his eyes. He knew she was right. Frair would have to be strong to save not only his mother but also his friends. He closed his eyes, trying to clear his mind. Suddenly the image of Cassy flashed in his mind, and he felt pain stab his heart.

"Is that the Champion?" Privlana asked.

"Yes, I hate to think of her facing the Evil Queen alone," Frair's heart ached for Cassy and the task ahead for her.

"Do not fear for her, my son. I have a good feeling about this Champion. Apparently, Alona fears her greatly, so I believe she will have the strength to be victorious."

Frair knew his Mother was probably correct, yet a part of him worried about Cassy's safety. He did not understand the feelings stirring up from deep inside of him, but for some unknown reason, she seemed to possess his heart.

"Mother, we have been able to speak by sharing our thoughts. Can we see each other as well?" He held his breath and waited for her answer.

Privlana felt her heart leap with joy at his request. "Yes, my son, but I must warn you I am not in my Dragon form."

"It does not matter, Mother. I just want to know you are real and not a product of my imagination. Seeing your face will give me the strength I need to face the danger ahead for me."

Frair felt a strange tingling in his head as the image of a beautiful woman with flaming red hair, and bright green eyes appeared before him in his mind.

"You're beautiful," the words escaped his mouth.

"And you are quite handsome, my son," Privlana cried with tears of joy.

"We both have the same green eyes," he laughed with the thrill of knowing they shared something special.

"Yes, all Dragons have eyes the color of emeralds. It is a sign of your Royal Heritage. Still, I must warn you they will glow blood red when we are angry. Your Father's were the brightest of all dragons," Privlana laughed softly as the memory of her beloved husband flowed into her mind.

Frair gasped. "Is that my father?"

Taken aback by the question, Privlana felt her heart quicken. "Can you see him? Oh, how wonderful; yes, that is your Father."

Frair squeezed his eyes tighter, trying to hold on to the vision in his mind. "Mother, I see flames dancing in his eyes. Why don't you or I have them?"

"What an excellent observation, my son. The flames dancing in your father's eyes show the intensity of his powers. Your eyes will have the same once you take his powers as King."

Frair felt sadness tug at his heart at never knowing his father and mother. "Mother, do you think Father would be proud of me?"

"Oh, yes, he was so excited about your coming birth. He would count the days until you came forth from the egg, as did I," Privlana's voice was soft and sorrowful at the memories of the loss of their lives together.

"So, you both wanted me? You didn't cast me away?"

Privlana sensed his sadness and wished she could take him in her arms. "Oh, my son, my heart has ached every day to see you. My heart broke to know you would come forth from the egg and not know about your heritage. Your father had such plans for you. He wanted to teach you the way of the Dragon and all the responsibilities involved. You are a Prince of Walandra and destined to be its King."

The words hit Frair with such force he could barely breathe. How could he be a King over the entire Kingdom? He could not even sleep in Roupert's hut without nearly burning it to the ground.

Privlana sensed his doubts and quickly tried to put his mind at ease. "Do not fear, my son. You will make a great King someday, but that day has not come yet. First, we must stop Alona from obtaining the Blood Key. The Champion is wearing the sacred Breast Plate and Blood Key, so she needs to come to me in the dungeon to break the curse Alona has over the kingdom. I sense great courage in Cassandra, and I know with the help of Roupert and Keira, the Milif, she will be triumphant. Do not surrender to doubt, my son, for we have the power of good on our side."

Frair knew she was correct, but he could not help but worry.

"Mother," he asked, with his eyes tightly closed.

"Yes, Frair," her voice was calm and reassuring.

"I'm glad you are alive and thank you for coming to me tonight," tears streamed down his cheeks again.

Privlana felt her heart warm with love and pride. "I'm so proud of you, and I look forward to the moment when I can take you in my arms. I love you, my son. Rest well, for tomorrow will be a difficult day for us all. Goodnight."

"I love you too, Mother and goodnight."

The swirling fog appeared again, this time taking the vision of Privlana from Frair's mind. Once she was gone, he relaxed against the cold wall, feeling a new sense of pride surge through him. He was glad to have learned the truth from his mother and to discover what she expected of him.

"I promise not to fail, Mother," his words filled the empty room as he realized there was no escape for what lies ahead of him and those he cared for.

Chapter 19

The morning sun gently kissed Cassy on the cheek, awakening her from her restless slumber.

"Good morning," Roupert said playfully. "I found some berries for our breakfast. I'm sure you didn't want to eat dried meat this early in the day."

"Berries sound fantastic, thank you." Cassy had to admit she was relieved not to be eating the dried meat again so soon.

Roupert handed her a small pouch of berries then sat next to her.

"Aren't you going to eat?" Cassy held the pouch out toward him.

"No, I ate while you were still sleeping. I've been awake for some time now going over our plans again," he smiled, but Cassy could see the concern in his eyes.

She reached into the pouch and pulled out a handful of the berries then shoved them into her mouth.

"These are really good," she grinned with berry juice flowing from the corners of her mouth.

"I'd say so," Roupert chuckled as he wiped the juice from her face with a small rag.

Once Cassy had swallowed the mouthful of berries, she shot Roupert a concerned look. "I'm worried."

"What worries you?" He thought he knew the answer, but he needed to know for sure.

"What if we can't do it? What if we fail to get the stone and breastplate to Queen Privlana?" Cassy lowered her head, trying to hide the shame burning in her heart.

Roupert reached out and took her hand in his. "I understand your fear, for I feel the same. We are facing great danger, and Alona will not hesitate to kill both of us to obtain the Blood Key. She is an evil soul, who only cares about her own power, so we must try to remain strong and have faith good always wins out over evil."

Cassy lifted her face and gazed into his eyes, seeing compassion and strength, staring back at her. "I hope you're right. You know something; I wish Melissa was here. Don't ever tell her I said this, but she's the smart one of the two of us. Melissa will never admit it, but she's level-headed and able to think her way out of trouble. She just acts like an airhead, so no one will expect anything of her. Me; I'm more the charge in before thinking things through sort of person. I can't tell you the times I've gotten into trouble for not stopping first and thinking before acting. I hate to admit it, but I kinda wish Melissa was here. That way the Queen could go after her, instead of me," Cassy glanced over at Roupert and grinned playfully.

Roupert could not help but laugh at the silly expression on her face. "Well, my young friend, I see great courage in you, and I believe we will be triumphant."

Roupert gave her hand a squeeze, this making her giggle. "I am glad you are the Champion, and you are here."

"I'm glad I'm here with you, too. The old Evil Queen may think she has us, but we will have a surprise for her. We're going to get the Blood Key back to Queen Privlana and restore the Kingdom. We're going to be heroes, and the subjects of Walandra will tell stories of our bravery for generations," Cassy sat up straight with a new sense of purpose burning in her eyes.

"Why don't you finish the berries then we will leave for the castle," Roupert urged with a playful grin.

Cassy looked at him and shrugged her shoulders then put another handful of the succulent berries in her mouth.

Roupert had stood and was gathering their things when they heard a small voice.

"We have come to help the Champion vanquish the Evil Queen Alona."

Cassy turned and saw three little creatures standing in the tall grass by the path leading to the castle. She examined them carefully and decided they looked like elves from her storybooks. They were about three feet tall, with long, pointy noses and pointed ears. The tallest of the three was the one speaking, so she assumed he was the leader.

"Who are you?" Cassy looked at Roupert then over to the creatures.

"They are Elim," Roupert said with a hint of mistrust in his voice.

"Yes, we are Elim. My name is Athrat, this is Tamrath, and that is Gillmer," he pointed toward the other two then bowed toward Cassy.

"Yes, we heard the Champion had come to challenge the Queen, so we wanted to offer our assistance," Tamrath said with a crooked smile.

"We came to help you with your quest," Gillmer added.

Cassy took a step forward, but Roupert took her by the arm. "Do not trust them. They are selfish creatures who only do things for their own benefit. I promise you they do not care about helping you. They are only here to line their pockets with reward."

Athrat grasped his chest as though in pain. "It pains my heart to hear you say such things, Roupert. We have only come to offer our assistance to the Champion. We have no desire for reward."

"Tis true, tis true," the other two chimed in with the same pained looks.

Roupert was about to protest again when Cassy held up her hand. "Stop arguing. I think it's quite honorable you have come to offer your help with my quest. I would like to accept your help but on one condition."

The three Elim exchanged glances, and then looked back to Cassy, each nodding their agreement.

"Cassy, no, you cannot trust them," Roupert protested. He threateningly stepped toward the Elim, but Cassy prevented his advance.

"Stop, Roupert, you need to trust me. If these three are telling the truth, then I will know, but if they are lying, they will face my wrath."

Roupert wondered what she was doing, but he decided to step back and trust her. Cassy stepped closer to the three Elim and bent down to look them directly in the eyes.

"Do you see this?" she said in a calm voice as she rubbed her hand across the Blood Key.

They all nodded nervously but said nothing.

"This is the Blood Key, and it is attached to the sacred Breast Plate. I wear this because I am the Champion, and through it, I have great powers. Do you understand my words?"

The three nodded their heads again with fear growing to a fevered pitch.

"At first, I didn't understand what I could do, but now I know." She placed her hand firmly on the Blood Key, causing it to begin to glow and vibrate.

Roupert watched Cassy, surprised to see her acting this way. He glanced over at the Elim, who now were backing away from Cassy with fear showing in their eyes.

Cassy closed her eyes and took a deep breath, this causing the Blood Key to glow like fire with what appeared to be flames shooting out of it from between her fingers. The Elim took another step back when Cassy opened her eyes and looked at them again, but now her eyes were bright emerald green with ribbons of flames swirling around in them.

The three Elim gasped and dropped to their knees, pleading for their lives. "Please, Champion. You have the spirit of the Dragon inside you. Please do not kill us."

Roupert gazed at Cassy, shocked by this turn of events. He had not seen eyes like that for many years. Not since he served King Ashlym.

"You have come to take the Blood Key for your own. I will not allow creatures such as you to take what is not yours. Now leave while you still have your miserable lives," a deep growl escaped Cassy's lips.

"Yes, your Majesty, we meant no disrespect," the three Elim bowed as they slowly backed away, not wanting to turn their backs on Cassy.

"I'm sure you did not. Now, leave my sight before I change my mind," Cassy took a step forward, causing the Elim to turn and run for their lives.

Once they were gone, Cassy turned to face Roupert. "Wow; that was weird."

Roupert ran his fingers through his hair as he shook his head. "I do not know what weird is, but it definitely was strange," he laughed nervously. "If I didn't know any better, I would have sworn that was King Ashlym."

Cassy shook her head, trying to understand what had just happened. "I think it was. I felt him with me, in me. That was incredible. I felt so strong, as though nothing or no one could hurt me."

Roupert gawked at her, trying to understand her words. "It isn't possible. King Ashlym died many years ago. He died by Alona's hand with a dagger through the heart."

"I know, but isn't his blood in this?" she placed her hand over the Blood Key.

"Yes, but…"

"Roupert, I know what I felt. Keira and the Lillients told me the Blood Key chose me to be the Champion, and I would have powers because of it. They said Alona forced a drop of the King's blood inside of the stone, right?"

He nodded his head, realizing there was much he did not understand about the power of the Dragons.

"I believe somehow the King is still alive because of his blood inside the stone. I think when Alona forced his blood inside the stone to trap his powers, she also trapped his soul. I felt him inside of me. I felt his power and strength. I know with his help, we will vanquish Alona forever." Her gaze met his, and he knew in that instant she spoke the truth.

Roupert could not contain his joy. He grabbed Cassy and pulled her into his arms, holding her tightly.

"Hey, you're squeezing me," she gasped, trying to catch her breath.

"Oh, I'm sorry," he released her, then he laughed at the silly expression on her face as she straightened her clothes.

"I wondered why the Elim were so terrified. When you threatened them, your eyes looked like King Ashlym's with ribbons of flames swirling in the bright emerald green. Your voice took on his tone, as well."

"I did? No wonder those three were ready to run for the hills," Cassy laughed a deep belly laugh, remembering the look of terror on their faces.

Roupert laughed as well. "I must admit I was frightened for a moment. However, I am no longer worried, for I know my King is watching over us. We have nothing to fear with him at our side."

"I feel the same way. Come on, let's go rescue Frair and save the Kingdom so Aaron and I can go home," Cassy said with a joyous tone in her voice.

Chapter 20

Privlana awoke feeling lightness in her heart, something she had not felt for many years. She had long prayed to see her son, but with each passing year, she had begun to lose hope.

"Frair, you are such a handsome young man," she whispered as she lay on the filthy straw mat on the dungeon floor.

"What did you say? Oh, you poor thing, you've been down here so long you are beginning to talk to yourself," Alona chuckled as she crossed the floor toward Privlana.

"I didn't say anything, you must be hearing things," Privlana shot back, not wanting Alona to know of her time with Frair the night before.

"If you say so, but I'm sure I heard you say something. No matter, I just wanted to come down and visit with you for a while. You see, today is going to be a special day for us both. Today, I will obtain the Blood Key and everyone you care for, including your sweet son, Frair will die. Yes, today is going to be a full day," Alona laughed devilishly.

"You are such a fool, Alona. You already tried once to get the power of the Blood Key and failed. What makes you believe you will be successful today?"

Alona stepped closer and lowered her voice. "Because I have your son, and if the Champion does not give me the Blood Key, then I will kill him, and that foolish Roupert, who travels with her."

Privlana had known Alona was desperate to get the Blood Key, but she never thought she would resort to killing Frair when she could harness his power as well, unless....

She doesn't know, Privlana quickly shoved the thought from her mind.

Alona lowered her eyes, trying to read Privlana's thoughts. "What are you thinking?"

"Nothing, I'm not of thinking anything other than what a pitiful creature you are," Privlana said flatly.

Alona did not appreciate Privlana's words and raised her hand in anger. "I should strike you dead now."

Privlana lifted her head and looked directly at Alona. "But you won't because it will prevent you from fulfilling your plans. We both know my death will forever keep the Blood Key out of your reach. You know that, as do I. So, lower your hand, and be gone, for I wish to be alone."

Privlana lay back down on the mat then turned her back to Alona.

"Enjoy this time, Privlana, for soon you and your son will join your husband in the Land of Shadows." Alona turned on her heel and walked back toward the stairway. She turned one last time to look again at Privlana, then in a huff, she stormed up the stairs and out of sight.

Once Alona was gone, Privlana closed her eyes and reached out to Frair. She had to warn him of Alona's intent.

***

Cassy and Roupert rolled up their blankets and put everything away in their packs. Once they knew they had everything, they both took a deep breath and walked toward the path leading through the woods to the rear side of the castle. Roupert had used the small door hidden in the tall bushes along the eastern wall of the castle when he helped Abigail on her quest. Most in the castle had no knowledge of the small door as it was only for the Royal family should they ever have a need to escape unseen.

"How much farther is the castle from here?" Cassy asked as she followed Roupert through the trees growing over the path and making it nearly impassable.

"It's not too far. If I remember correctly, it's less than an hour's walk from here."

"Dang, you'd think Keira could have dropped us somewhere a little closer," Cassy snickered at the surprised look on Roupert's face.

"True, but we wouldn't want the Queen's men to have found us sleeping while they were out on patrol, would we?" He then laughed at the look of surprise on her face.

"No, I guess Keira knew what she was doing, after all," Cassy grumbled as she pushed another low hanging branch out of her way.

They had walked in silence for several minutes until Cassy spoke again, "Roupert?"

"Yes, what is on your mind?" He sensed something was bothering her.

"Do you believe Alona will hurt Frair?" Just the thought of him held captive by the evil Alona made Cassy nauseous.

Roupert did not want to tell her the truth, but he knew he must. He swallowed and steadied himself before answering.

"I'm afraid she would. She craves the Power of the Dragon above all else, and she will stop at nothing to obtain it for her own. Her heart is dark and full of evil, so she will not hesitate to kill anyone who stands in her way."

"I was worried about that."

Roupert looked over his shoulder and smiled at her. "Do not worry, though. I have faith in you, Cassy. Yesterday when the Elim tried to trick you, you showed real strength. I felt as though I was in the presence of King Ashlym again."

Cassy stopped in her tracks, touched by his words. "I have to admit I felt him there with me. He was so powerful. I could feel him surging through me."

Roupert turned around to face her. "I don't understand what happened, but I believe he was there with you. When I looked into your eyes, I saw him there. Your eyes changed to the color of the Royal Emerald Green, with the same swirling ribbons of flames that burned in King Ashlym's eyes. I don't understand how it happened, but your voice even sounded like the King."

Cassy searched for the words to express her thoughts, but none came to her.

Roupert saw the look on her face and understood her emotions. "Come on, Champion. We have a Kingdom to save."

He turned around and began walking through the trees toward the castle.

"Hurry up," he released a tree branch blocking the path. "Watch out."

Cassy quickly ducked under the tree branch before it struck her. "Hey, that wasn't nice," she scolded.

"I was just testing your reflexes," Roupert teased.

"Maybe I need to walk in front and test your reflexes," Cassy retorted with a wicked grin on her face.

Roupert waved his hand over his shoulder as he continued down the path. "My reflexes are just fine, but stay close, for we are near the castle."

Cassy's breath caught in her throat at the thought they were almost there. She reached up and touched the Blood Key and felt its warmth under her fingertips.

"I sure hope you're still with me, King Ashlym," her voice was a near whisper.

Roupert glanced back at her. "Did you say something?"

"No, I was just thinking aloud." Cassy wanted to tell him the truth, but something held her back.

"We need to be careful from now on. We don't wish to alert the castle guards." Roupert glanced over his shoulder and gave her a reassuring smile.

As they got closer to the castle, Cassy felt the Blood Key begin to vibrate. She reached up and touched it, feeling a strange sensation surge into her hand then up her arm. Next, her body started to feel warm, and every nerve in her body seemed to come alive.

Do not fear, my child, for I am with you," a gentle voice filled her mind, and she suddenly realized the fear she had felt moments before was now gone.

Is that you, King Ashlym? The question formed in her mind, awaiting an answer she was unsure she would receive.

Yes, and I am pleased you have come, Cassandra. I have waited many years for one with the strength and courage I see in you.

Cassy felt his power surge through her body. *I don't understand something. Everyone says you're dead. They say Alona killed you, but you can't be dead because I feel you here with me.* Cassy reached up and wiped a tear from her eye.

There is much misunderstanding regarding the Power of the Dragon. There are many levels of magic that few know to exist. Once we have vanquished Alona, I promise to share everything with you, but now you must stay focused on the task ahead, for you are near to the castle.

Roupert stopped and turned to face Cassy. "The castle is not far ahead. I want you to stay here while I go see if there are any guards nearby."

Cassy nodded her head then sat on a fallen tree. "Be careful, and don't forget to come back to get me," she replied nervously.

Roupert gave her a playful wink as he turned and disappeared through the thick overgrowth. Cassy looked around at the trees, wondering what the day would bring. Would they rescue Frair and free Queen Privlana, or would Alona defeat them?

She closed her eyes, trying to clear her thoughts when she heard a small voice whisper in her ear.

"Do not fear, Cassandra. I have been watching over you this entire time. I know you will be victorious this day, so put your fears aside," Keira spoke in a hushed tone.

Cassy opened her eyes and saw the tiny Milif hovering in front of her. "It's good to see you again, Keira."

"How are you feeling today?" Keira asked with a playful tone in her voice.

Cassy looked at Keira, wondering how she could ask such a strange question. "You want to know how I'm feeling? Well, let's see, I'm trapped in a strange world with a Dragon's Breast Plate and a gemstone with the blood of the King of the Dragon's trapped inside of it. Then, I have an Evil Queen wanting to steal the stone, and she's willing to kill me in the process. Just how do you think I feel?"

Keira's expression was replaced with one of sadness when she answered Cassy. "That was not the answer I had hoped to hear."

"I don't understand. What do you want me to say?"

Keira reached out and touched the Blood Key. "Why do you deny what you feel?"

Cassy's eyes lit up with excitement. "You know. You know King Ashlym lives inside of the Blood Key, don't you?"

Keira nodded; surprised Cassy would even question this. "Of course, I do. I have served the King for thousands of years. I knew the day Alona forced his blood inside of the Blood Stone, she had also trapped his spirit. She would have certainly controlled his power had Queen Privlana not cast the spell that transformed the Blood Stone into a key."

Cassy listened intently as Keira explained everything to her.

"I did not feel the King's spirit when Abigail came to Walandra. While she was brave, it was not her destiny to free us from Alona's curse. Everything changed when you appeared, though. I felt the Blood Key's powers and those of King Ashlym."

"Do you believe I can defeat Alona? She is so powerful, and…"

Keira held up her hand. "Yes, it is true that her powers are great, but you have the Power of the Dragon. There no power greater in this realm. Today will be a great day for the subjects of Walandra, and you will prove your bravery. I must give you a warning. Alona will use trickery, so trust your heart, not your eyes. She will use your love for your brother as well as your friendship with Roupert and Frair. Surrender to the Power of the Dragon, and you will be victorious. I must go, Roupert returns." Keira vanished in a ball of shimmering light.

The sound of footsteps brought Cassy to attention. She held her breath as she waited for Roupert. After a few moments, he appeared through the thick overgrowth.

"It is clear for us to go. Hurry, we need to get inside the castle before the next patrol."

Cassy quickly got to her feet and followed Roupert toward the castle and her destiny.

***

Frair sat in the corner of the dark and dank room with only the light of the sun peeking through the small window high above his head. He had tried to sleep but without success, as the sound of his mother's voice kept replaying in his mind.

"How could things have gone so wrong?"

Frair thought back to his time with Roupert and all the happy memories they shared. He had always thought of Roupert as a father, so when the Demlins told him his life was a lie, his heart had died a bit at hearing those painful words. Shame filled his heart at believing their lie.

"I'm sorry for not having more faith in you, Roupert. I was a foolish child to have trusted them." Feeling despair, he closed his eyes with the image of his mother appearing in his mind.

"You are so beautiful." His heart leaped with joy as he held onto the image for as long as he could.

"Who is beautiful?" David chuckled as he appeared in the room.

"I wonder if he's thinking of Roupert. While he is not entirely dreadful-looking, I would not go as far to say he is beautiful," Ralph laughed as well when he appeared next to David.

Frair cringed when he heard their taunts, for he was in no mood to face them. All he wanted was to enjoy the memories of his time with his mother.

"Open your eyes and look upon us," David demanded in a dark and menacing tone.

Frair refused to do as commanded. He turned his face away and held his eyes tightly closed without saying a word.

David and Ralph were surprised by how the young Prince showed no fear of his current situation.

"So, the little Prince is feeling brave this morning. I wonder what could have happened to bring about this change in him?" Ralph growled with a look of contempt on his face.

"I do not know, but it's not a wise thing to do. Queen Alona will not be pleased with his attitude this morning," David chuckled at seeing Frair squeeze his eyes even tighter.

"Enjoy these last few moments of bravery, young Prince. The time of your usefulness grows short, and you will finally get to meet your loving mother." Ralph laughed when he saw Frair turn his head and look directly at him.

Frair felt the blood boil in his veins at the arrogant attitude of these two demonic creatures. He knew they had the upper hand for now, but something deep inside of him told him their plans for him, and his mother would fail.

"Enjoy this moment, for you will know defeat by my hands this day," Frair said in a calm yet firm voice.

David and Ralph found this comment quite amusing considering the situation in which the young Prince currently found himself.

"You are a foolish child," David fought to contain his laughter.

"Yes, he is," Ralph chimed in.

The Demlins gazes met, and at that moment, they could no longer contain their enjoyment of the current events.

Frair watched the two Demlins, and he wished he could turn them to ash with one burst of fire.

Frair fought to control his anger, and then he said in a calm voice, "Go ahead and laugh. I am the son of the mighty King Ashlym, King of the Dragons, and sole heir to the throne of Walandra. I will not allow Alona to rule over this kingdom for another day. It all ends today. I will see her cast into the Land of Shadows, along with all those who serve her. So, go ahead and laugh as you will be returning to the Land of Shadows along with your Queen today. Let her rule the subjects there."

Frair's face transformed, it was now something dark and foreboding, which made the Demlins question their own power. How could the young Prince speak such words? He was the prisoner of Queen Alona, not the other way around. Yet, they had to admit they saw something in his eyes to make them take pause.

Frair could see the doubt in their eyes, which only empowered him more. "I see the fear in your eyes. What is wrong, do you question your Queen's power?"

"We do not question our Queen's power over one as pitiful as you, young Prince. You are the one shackled in this dark room, away from everyone you hold dear," David countered defiantly.

Frair's eyelids lowered in a menacing glare. "Go ahead and enjoy these last moments, for you and your Queen will soon rue her attack on the Royal Family. She may have killed my father and enslaved my mother in the dungeon below, but today she will discover the real Power of the Dragon."

Fear now replaced victory in the eyes of the Demlins.

"How can it be he knows Queen Alona killed King Ashlym?" David tried to control his fear.

"There is no way he could know," Ralph stepped back from Frair with dread consuming him.

"Is that fear, I see glowing in your eyes? Frair teased.

The Demlins exchanged glances, with a mixture of both fear and disbelief showing on their faces.

Frair released a loud laugh that filled the small room. "You and your Queen have made the fatal mistake of underestimating the Power of the Dragon. I must tell you it will lead to your demise and that of your Queen."

David and Ralph were at a loss of how to respond. They knew the Power of the Dragon was the most powerful magic in all the realms, but the curse cast by Queen Alona had prevented any Dragon from using their powers. Queen Privlana sat in the dungeon trapped in her human form, as the rest of the Dragon clan sat atop the castle as stone Centurions. They sat in silence, overlooking the Kingdom from the spell cast by Privlana to save them from death.

Frair watched as doubt continued to grow in their eyes. "Ah, not so sure of victory now, are you?"

"We have nothing more to say to you. Prepare to do as commanded by Queen Alona, and maybe she will allow you to live," Ralph snarled dismissively.

Without saying another word, the two Demlins vanished in a puff of black smoke.

Once they were gone, Frair said a silent prayer his words were true, and this day would be the end of Alona's rule over Walandra.

Chapter 21

Roupert and Cassy reached the clearing along the back of the castle. She nervously looked around then followed Roupert to some tall bushes growing beside the castle wall.

"The door is behind these bushes." Roupert moved some of the branches aside, exposing a wooden door. "Hurry, we do not want to be seen by any guards who may be on patrol."

Roupert grasped the door handle and tugged. "It's stuck. Quick, help me pull on it."

Cassy rushed to his side and grabbed the handle, and together they gave it another tug. The door opened some, but not enough to fit through.

"Pull hard again," Roupert groaned.

Cassy braced herself, and when Roupert gave the order, she pulled with all her might.

With a loud groan, the door swung wide. Roupert glanced over at Cassy, who was smiling.

"Good job, now let us hope it closes much easier," Roupert winked.

They both stepped through the door, and Roupert quickly pulled it shut behind them.

"See, I told you we are a good team," he chuckled.

"True, but I was worried the door was stuck shut," Cassy teased.

"As was I, I guess the years had rusted the hinges in place, but together we were able to solve the problem. Let me see if I can find one of the torches they used to have along the wall."

Roupert began to rub his hand along the wall until he felt where they had left a torch. He removed it and then laid it on the stone floor. Next, he pulled the bronze-handled Firesteel and the knife hanging from his belt. Cassy watched intently as he leaned down and rested the Firesteel against the torch, struck his knife on the edge of the Firesteel, causing it to spark. It amazed her how the torch had caught fire after only three strikes and was now lighting up the small room.

"Wow. That was cool. I've never seen anyone start a fire like that before," Cassy shook her head from side-to-side in disbelief.

Roupert looked up at Cassy, confused by her response. "I do not understand. How do you start fires in your realm?"

"We have matches and lighters."

"What are matches and lighters?" Roupert asked.

Cassy thought for a moment before answering. "Well, matches are small sticks with a ball on the end of it that when you strike it on something rough, it causes a flame. I guess it sort of works on the same principle of your instrument by using friction to cause the fire."

Roupert nodded his head, understanding her explanation.

"Now a lighter is a device that uses fuel and a small flint. You push a button, which causes the striker to hit the flint, igniting the fuel inside of the lighter. That one is my favorite. I wish I had one, so I could show you."

"That sounds interesting, but I will stay with what I know. Come, we must go."

Roupert and Cassy headed down the long hallway that led deep into the castle. Cassy marveled how the torch caused strange-looking shadows to move along the walls, and she wondered if they were, in fact only shadows.

After several minutes, they came to a turn in the hallway, where they noticed light glowing from that direction.

"Wait here. I will go and make sure it is clear." Roupert handed her the torch.

Cassy did not like the idea of him leaving her behind, but she did as told. Roupert glanced back and gave her a playful wink. "I promise I won't be too long."

"Okay, but I want you to know I'll be counting the seconds," she teased.

Roupert reached out and gently touched her cheek. He then turned and vanished around the corner leaving Cassy standing there alone.

"Please don't forget me," she said silently to herself.

***

It had been many years since Roupert had walked the dark hidden hallways of the castle. As he slowly approached the light shimmering ahead of him, he wondered what waited for him and Cassy. He knew danger awaited them, and their chance of success was limited, but a voice inside of him kept telling him to believe. With each step, the light grew brighter until he finally reached the opening into a large room. He was about to enter the room when a voice filled his mind.

Stop; do not enter the room without Cassandra. She must be with you.

Who are you? How do I know I can trust you? Roupert answered in his mind, as he felt his heart pounding in his chest.

Has it been so long that you have forgotten me, Sir Roupert? He felt great sorrow suddenly fill his being, causing tears to come to his eyes.

My Queen, is that you? His heart raced with anticipation.

Yes, Sir Roupert, it is I, Queen Privlana. I have waited so long for this day. My heart is full of joy at knowing my time of bondage will soon end.

Roupert's heart leaped with joy at hearing her voice again, but then the image of Frair appeared in his mind. *My Queen, I have failed you. I did not protect the Prince from Alona. She has taken him.*

Do not fear for Frair. He is safe and now knows who he is. I want to thank you for raising him into an exceptional young man. Now, go bring Cassandra with you for your path ahead grows dangerous.

Roupert returned to where he had left, Cassy. Once there, he told her of his conversation with Queen Privlana and of how Frair was unharmed.

"Oh, thank goodness," Cassy cried out. "Well, let's do as the Queen ordered. Let's go kick some Evil Queen butt," she said with an excited gleam in her eyes.

Roupert bowed his head with a broad smile on his face, "As you command, my Champion."

Roupert took the torch from Cassy and laid it on the floor next to the wall. "We'll leave this here in case we need it for a hasty retreat."

Cassy flashed a confident and wicked grin. "We will not be retreating today. We are going to free Frair and his mother, then we will restore your kingdom. I plan to go home with Aaron, but we can't do it if we don't take down Alona and her evil followers. So, get any idea of failure out of your mind. The only person who must worry today is Alona."

***

The sound of murmuring alerted Roupert and Cassy of danger ahead. They exchanged concerned glances then prepared for their attack. The two guards standing at the door leading to the main hall had no warning, as Roupert and Cassy made their presence known. Before either could reach for his sword, Roupert had slain one with his sword, and the other with his knife.

"Wow, you really are a great knight," Cassy proclaimed excitedly.

Roupert shook his head as he replaced his sword and knife to their sheaths. "I did not enjoy taking their lives, Cassandra. One does not feel joy when killing a man, he once called a friend."

Cassy saw the sorrow in his eyes and understood his words. "I'm sorry. I didn't know."

Roupert looked into her eyes, feeling her pain. "You have no reason to apologize. Alona had cast a spell over them, so they were no longer the brave and loyal men I once knew. I'm sure we will face many more as we continue on our way to the dungeon to rescue Queen Privlana."

Cassy knew he was right, but she did not fully understand what they were facing until this moment. She glanced down at the two slain men and said a silent prayer she and Roupert would not meet the same fate.

"Come, we must hurry before it is time to change the guards." Roupert took her by the hand and pulled her along with him.

***

They had quickly moved down the long hallway until they came to a large door covered with strange carvings. Roupert stopped in front of the door and drew in a deep breath.

"What's wrong? Where does that door lead to?" All of a sudden, Cassy felt a sensation of dread mixed with excitement surge through her.

"It is the door to the dungeon," Roupert said flatly.

Cassy looked up at him and shook her head. "But that's good, right?"

Roupert closed his eyes, searching for the right words to say. "Yes, it is a good thing, but we must also realize Alona has undoubtedly set a trap for us once we enter this door. We must release all fear and doubt from our hearts and minds. We must stand united against her, as that will be the only way we will be victorious. You must rely on the power of the Blood Key to guide you."

Cassy saw the concern in his eyes and had to admit she was feeling the same way. She reached up and gently brushed her fingertips against the Blood Key, and suddenly felt a great power enter her body.

"Do not fear, Roupert. Today we will end the rule of Alona. She shall be cast to the Land of Shadows, where she will suffer for all eternity," Cassy spoke in a profound and powerful voice.

Roupert stepped back, surprised by her change in mood as well as the tone of her voice. "Cassandra..."

When their gazes met, Roupert saw the same emerald green eyes with ribbons of fire dancing in them he saw the day before.

"King Ashlym, is that you?" Roupert felt his heart leap with joy at knowing the King was with them.

"Yes, Sir Roupert, I am with Cassandra. I am pleased the Blood Key chose her, for she has much courage within her."

Roupert watched as Cassy's eyes returned to their normal color, and the look on her face softened.

"Are you alright?" He asked when she shook her head and blinked her eyes several times.

"Am I alright? I've never felt better. That is so cool. I can feel him with me. I felt him some last night when I chased off those three Elim, but nothing like I do today. I'm no longer afraid. I'm ready to face Alona and send her to the Land of Shadows." Cassy squared her shoulders; confident they would be victorious.

Roupert was both surprised and pleased with this development. He knew they were facing great danger, so to know King Ashlym was with them, eased his fears. He reached for the door handle then glanced over his shoulder at Cassy. "There is no going back now. Prepare yourself to face your worst nightmare."

With that, he swung the door wide and stepped inside with Cassy following closely behind.

Chapter 22

Neither was prepared for what awaited them inside the dungeon. Across the large room was Queen Privlana, bound in chains and hanging in mid-air. Cassy struggled to see what they had secured the chain to, but it just seemed to disappear into nothingness.

"Sir Roupert, please stop, it's a trap," Privlana cried out.

All of a sudden, from a dark corner of the room, ominous laughter broke out. "Yes, Sir Roupert, it is a trap. I must say I am pleased to see you have brought the Champion with you as well."

"Alona!" Just the sound of her voice made him burn with rage.

"How disrespectful of you to refer to me in such a manner; I am your Queen, and you should refer to me as such," Alona demanded with an angry tone in her voice.

Roupert stepped forward, holding his head high. "You are NOT my Queen. You have unjustly enslaved the true Queen of Walandra, and for that, you shall pay."

Alona laughed at his stubbornness and foolish loyalty.

"Roupert, you never cease to amaze me. After all these years, you are still loyal to a dead

King and his pitiful wife. The time of the Dragon is over. They are nothing more than a faded memory of a time long ago." Alona flicked her hand toward Privlana, this causing her to cry out in pain as the chains tightened around her body.

Consumed with rage, Roupert charged forward with his sword held firmly in his hand. "Stop; stop hurting her, or I will kill you!"

"My, how brave you are, Roupert," Alona laughed wickedly.

Roupert began to move toward Alona when Cassy stepped forward, showing herself.

"Awe, there you are. I have long awaited our meeting, Cassandra, the Champion, arrives to end my reign. It is true; you do look like your great-grandmother. Yet, I do sense something different about you. Yes, something different in the eyes."

Cassy stood in place with her gaze firmly locked on Alona, "As I have waited to meet you. Don't even dare to believe for a second you're going to win our little battle. I plan to knock you right off your Royal Throne and then send you to the Land of Shadows where you belong. Who knows, maybe you can rule there as their Queen. Walandra already has a Queen, and it sure isn't you," Cassy grinned when she saw the smug look on Alona's face transform into one of rage.

"Oh, look, I think I've upset her," Cassy hit Roupert on the arm with her elbow.

Alona lifted her arm in a fit of rage, causing a ball of red fire to appear in her hand. "You will die for your insolence," she hissed as she released the flaming ball.

The ball of flames soared through the air, spiraling and shooting flames in all directions. Roupert watched helplessly, as it flew past him and went directly at Cassy.

Cassy never blinked or moved as the flames moved toward her then as it was about to consume her, she held out her hand and caused the flames to disappear.

"NO, that is impossible," Alona shouted in disbelief. Alona held up her hand again, this time creating an even larger ball of fire. She then released the ball and waited.

This time, Roupert stepped in front of the ball of fire, and then fell to the ground, clutching his chest.

"NO, Roupert, please don't die," Cassy screamed as she knelt down, touching him on the forehead.

"Oh, my, how brave of him to sacrifice himself for you. It's a shame it will all be for not," Alona voiced with mocked sincerity.

As Cassy leaned over Roupert, she felt rage begin to grow from deep inside of her. She reached for the Blood Key and gently brushed her fingers over it, feeling the same warm sensation. Cassy's heart ached, refusing to accept Roupert was dead. As the warm feeling surged through her body, she reached down and rested her hand on Roupert's chest. She closed her eyes and felt an intense power growing deep inside of her.

What happened next would be told to the children of Walandra for many years to come. As Cassy's hand rested on Roupert's chest, it began to glow a bright and fiery red. She held her hand to his chest until a bright, sparkling light engulfed his entire body, and time seemed to stand still, as no one in the dungeon moved.

"You will live," Cassy commanded with a deep tone in her voice.

She pressed her hand firmly on his chest again, and in a flash of light, his lungs filled with breath, and his eyes fluttered open.

"Cassandra," Roupert whispered as he fought to gain his senses.

Cassy looked down at Roupert, and then tenderly stroked his forehead. "You're going to be alright. Stay here, I have to take care of a little problem."

"What have you done?" Alona shouted. Alona felt a growing fear consume her. She had never expected this young girl to have the ability to control the Blood Key with such skill.

Cassy stood and glared at Alona. "I have come to restore the throne to the rightful rulers. Your days of rule are over, and I will make you pay for your treachery. I will give you the opportunity to step aside or find yourself forever banished to the Land of Shadows."

Alona scowled at Cassy, who stood unyielding before her. "You, foolish child, I have powers you can never imagine. Today, it will be you and your pitiful friends who will find yourselves banished. I am Queen, and I will rule Walandra forever! Bring the young Prince here."

Cassy's blood turned to ice when she watched two guards appear from the shadows leading Frair, who was bound in chains. His gaze met Cassy's, and in that instant, she realized the fear she felt at seeing Roupert lying on the cold, stone floor was now an uncontrollable rage.

"Cassy..." he shouted while trying to free himself from the chains snuggly secured around his wrists and ankles.

"Quiet!" Alona ordered with a flick of her hand, causing his words to catch in his throat.

Watching Frair struggle against the hold that Alona had over him, awakened a power inside of Cassy that consumed her entire being. "Leave him alone!"

Alona saw the anger burning in her eyes. "He is mine to do with as I wish. You do not have the power to stop me."

Alona lifted her hand again. Frair's gaze met Cassy's, and in that instant, he floated into the air.

"If you want to save the young Prince, bring me the Blood Key," Alona's voice took on a low and threatening tone.

Cassy watched as more guards now stepped from the shadows. "No, you will never possess the Blood Key. I am the Champion, and through its power, I will destroy you."

Alona's eyes narrowed, "I said, give me the Blood Key, or the Prince dies!"

Alona flicked her hand toward Frair again and brought forth agonizing cries of pain. "Please, do not surrender, Cassy," he cried out as pain consumed his body.

Cassy suddenly realized two guards were closing in on her from the doorway. She reached up and brushed her fingertips across the Blood Key, causing it to glow a vibrant red.

What happened next surprised Alona. She stood in stunned silence as Cassy whirled about to face her attackers with a fire burning in her eyes. The guards charged toward her with their swords held high, and before either of them could react, they vanished in a puff of smoke.

"What have you done?" Alona screeched as she began to feel uncertainty about her future as Queen.

Before Cassy could answer, two more guards advanced on her. She turned to face them, and in an instant, they vanished as the two before them.

Consumed with anger and fear, Alona searched her mind for what to do. She knew if she did not act quickly, the Champion would slay all of her guards and leave her unprotected.

"Stand down, your time of rule is over," Cassy said in a dark and threatening tone. She glanced down at Roupert, letting him know she had things under control.

"You silly child, I will never surrender the throne. Do you not see I have the Prince and Queen under my control? If you do not want to see their deaths today, then give me the Blood Key!"

Alona raised her hand then released a strange glowing ball that enveloped Privlana, causing her to cry out in pain.

"Stop it. Stop hurting her." Cassy shook with anger. She knew she had to act quickly, or Alona would kill the Queen.

Cassy looked around the large room and noticed several guards advancing on her.

"Cassandra, you can't take all of them by yourself. Let me help," Roupert groaned as he struggled to his feet.

"How will you best my guards and save the Queen and Prince at the same time?" Alona taunted as she flicked her hand toward Frair, causing him to cry out in pain.

Cassy's mind was spinning. She looked at Queen Privlana and then to Frair. She saw the pain in their eyes, and she worried Alona would kill them regardless if she gave her the Blood Key.

"Cassy, we must act now!" Roupert withdrew his sword and held it out toward the approaching guards

Suddenly, Cassy felt the power of the Blood Key surge through her body. She then turned and faced Roupert. "Sir Roupert, wield your mighty sword and protect the Champion," Cassy said in a deep voice with sparks of flames dancing in her emerald green eyes.

"King Ashlym?" Roupert whispered.

Not prepared for what happened next, Alona gasped with disbelief. Cassy placed her hand on the Blood Key then rested her hand on Roupert's shoulder, causing him to glow with a fiery flame consuming his entire body. He then turned and faced the approaching guards, holding his sword at the ready.

Alona watched in horror as Roupert stuck down her guards. His body shimmered with the red glow, and one by one, the guards fell to the floor.

"How is that possible?" Alona growled.

Cassy slowly approached Alona as the battle raged around her. Her eyes glowed with intensity as she seemed possessed by a powerful force.

Alona turned to face Cassy with fear and anger burning in her eyes. "You will die!"

Alona lifted her arm, and a ball of fire appeared in the palm of her hand. She released an evil laugh then threw the fireball at Cassy, gleefully awaiting the demise of this Champion. As the fireball flew across the room, a strange shimmering light surrounded Cassy in a protective bubble.

Shock and anger consumed Alona as she watched the sparkling light around Cassy absorb the fireball, removing its destructive power.

"How can that be?" Alona screamed with disbelief and rage.

Alona watched everything playing out before her and realized she was losing the battle. Roupert had slain most of her guards, and Cassy was steadily advancing on her. She glanced over at Privlana, who still hung in the air, bound in chains.

"Please, stop this," Privlana pleaded.

"Stop? I will not stop until I have the Blood Key," Alona hissed in a threatening tone.

Alona turned and faced Frair. "Maybe I will just kill the young Prince and end the reign of the Dragons now."

Alona raised her arm when Cassy shouted, "Stop, Alona! You will not harm him."

"You dare speak to me in such a manner? I am a Queen, and I will not have a lowly creature as you talk to me in such a manner. I will do as I please, and there is nothing you can do to stop me."

"That is where you are wrong, Alona. For I have something you desire," Cassy looked at Alona with her eyes shimmering a bright emerald green and flames swirling around in them. Cassy reached up and tapped the Breast Plate twice by the Blood Key, opening the small door hiding the vial containing the nectar from the blossom of the Samen plant.

"I have the power to end your rule in my hand. It was a special gift from my friend, Othan," Cassy said as she removed the vial and held it up for Alona to see.

"Why should I fear anything a foolish old man gave you?" Alona prodded dismissively.

Cassy was pleased to see the doubt in Alona's eyes betray her words. She then opened the vial and swallowed its contents, feeling the power of the flower fill her body.

Alona was shocked, as Cassy seemed to transform before her eyes. Realizing she must act quickly, Alona turned to Frair and raised her arm. "You will now die, young Prince."

Nothing could have prepared Alona for what happened next.

"By the power of the nectar of the Samen plant and that of the Dragon, I release you from the spell of protection cast by your mother, Queen Privlana." Cassy raised her arms toward Frair, and in a flash of light, his chains broke and fell to the floor.

"How is this possible?" Alona cried out as the once small and helpless Dragon transformed into a great and fearsome Dragon, breathing fire, and smoke from his mouth and nostrils.

"NO, that is impossible," Alona shouted, barely able to contain her fear.

Frair released a mighty roar as he spread his massive wings. "You have destroyed my family, and caused great suffering to the subjects of Walandra, Alona. You betrayed the trust my parents had in you for your evil desire for power, but all that ends today."

Alona did not notice that Cassy was now standing beside Privlana.

Privlana looked down at Cassy and saw her eyes. "Ashlym, is that you?" She gasped breathlessly, as the pain of the chains, crushing her body consumed her.

Cassy looked up at Privlana and said with joy on her face, "Yes, it is I, my dearest. Today we will be together again."

At hearing these words, Alona turned and was caught off guard by what she saw. "No, it is not possible. You are dead, I killed you! Do you want to be reunited with your precious wife? Fine, here she is."

Alona pointed her finger at Privlana and began to speak the words of a death curse."

Rage and the desire for revenge overtook Frair. He roared again, causing Alona to break her train of thought and look at him.

"By the Power of the Dragon, I cast you into the deepest depths of the Land of Shadows, where you shall be imprisoned for all time." Red flames shot forth from Frair and enveloped Alona in a fiery ball of light.

"No, I will not surrender! I will not go!" Alona shouted as she fought against the force, dragging her down into the dark and fear-filled depths of the Land of Shadows.

"Begone, Evil Queen. Go rule the Demlins, Ralph, and David in your new kingdom," Frair laughed with joy as he watched her disappear in a bright green flash of light.

Once Alona was gone, the remainder of the guards fighting Roupert dropped their swords in surrender.

"It is over, the rule of Alona is over!" the guards shouted with glee.

Roupert dropped his sword as he stepped forward to greet his old friends. "Dalmen, my old friend, it is good to see you," Roupert grabbed Dalmen had hugged him enthusiastically with tears of joy in his eyes.

Dalmen cried on Roupert's shoulder as shame overtook him. "I'm sorry for my betrayal. I just couldn't stop myself…"

Roupert released Dalmen and looked directly into his eyes. "Do not feel as though you betrayed me, my old friend. Alona bewitched you, so nothing you have done is your fault. I only wish I did not have to kill our brothers."

Roupert looked around at the slain guards, feeling sadness grip his heart.

A fearsome growl drew Roupert's attention away from Dalmen and the other guards. "Oh my," he said in disbelief.

The vision of Frair surprised Roupert. While Frair resembled his father in stature and looks, Roupert could see the gentle spirit of his mother in him as well.

"Mother," Frair cried out as he stepped closer to where Privlana now lay on the stone floor. Once Frair had cast Alona into the Land of Shadows, the spell holding Privlana bound in chains was broken.

Cassy was already at her side, holding her hand.

"My son, you have done it. You have rid the Kingdom of Alona. I had always believed the Champion would be the one to do it. On the other hand, I am pleased it was you. I do fear my time with you grows short. I feel the cold hands of death pulling on my soul," Privlana whispered.

"No, I cannot lose you. I just found you," he cried out, with loud wails of pain.

"It is not your time to go, my love," the deep voice of Ashlym escaped from Cassy's lips.

Frair's gaze met Cassy's, and he was surprised to see her eyes shimmer a bright emerald green with swirling flames dancing in them.

"Who are you?" the words escaped his mouth before he realized what he had said.

Roupert stepped up next to Frair and smiled. "That is the spirit of your father, King Ashlym. He has been with Cassandra from the moment she wore the Blood Key."

"I don't understand. How is that possible?" Frair shook his head, finding it difficult to believe this news.

Cassy placed her hand on the Breast Plate. "Son, there is much you do not know about the Power of the Dragon. You see, your mother will not die today."

Cassy grasped the Breast Plate, and the straps holding it in place disappeared. She then held it out, and to Roupert's and Frair's surprise, it transformed from the stone plate into a Dragon breast scale with the Blood Key still attached to the center.

"Step back," Cassy said with a glint in her eyes. She then positioned Privlana on her back and gently laid the scale on Privlana's chest.

A strange vibration filled the room, making Roupert and Frair take several steps back.

"What is going on?" Frair asked as he watched the breast scale shimmer a bright green with bursts of flames shooting from the Blood Key.

The magic of the Blood Key filled the room, making everyone feel its power surge through them like bolts of lightning. Several of the guards dropped to their knees in fear, while Roupert and Dalmen bowed with reverence.

Suddenly, a green fog surrounded Privlana, lifting her from the floor. Her long red hair fluttered in the air as she spun slowly with beams of bright light emanating from her fingertips and toes.

Time stood still, as Frair watched the transformation of his mother from her human form into the beautiful image of the Dragon now standing before him.

Frair, my beloved son," she cried out to him.

Joy filled Frair's heart, as it seemed to soar among the clouds. "Mother," he cried, tears wetting his cheeks.

Privlana reached up and touched the breastplate once again, covering her chest above her mighty Dragon's heart.

"It is over. The curse is broken," she cried, feeling joy and peace overtake her.

Cassy stepped forward and looked up at Privlana. "It's not over. There is one more thing you must do, but it will take the love you and Frair share to complete this task."

Cassy held out her hand. When she opened her fingers, everyone in the room gasped when they saw the Blood Stone resting in the palm of her hand. "Your Majesty, Frair, you both must close your eyes and visualize King Ashlym in your minds. You must harness all of your love and power to complete this last task."

Cassy stood between Privlana and Frair and held out the Blood Stone. The guards were huddled together, unsure of what was about to happen, and Roupert eyes were wide with anticipation as he held his breath.

The room was deathly quiet. Cassy lifted the Blood Stone above her head and shouted in a clear voice, "Come forth, by the Power of the Dragon. I call ye from the Land of Shadows to the Land of the Living."

Roupert stood in stunned amazement, as a powerful light came forth from the Blood Stone and filled the entire room. Everything seemed to move as in the rippling of water, and Roupert felt his mind grow faint.

The guards feared for their lives, as the light seemed to consume them like fire in a pit. At the final moment, when all hope was lost, a significant cracking noise filled the dungeon, and in a massive cloud of smoke, the mighty Dragon, King Ashlym appeared.

"My love," Queen Privlana cried out with joy.

"My King," Roupert and the guards shouted with glee as they dropped to one knee, bowing with reverence.

King Ashlym turned and faced Frair. "My son, it is good to see you," he smiled when he saw tears fill Frair's eyes.

"Oh, Father," Frair cried, his heart filled with joy.

King Ashlym then turned and faced Cassy. "I owe you a great debt, Cassandra. You have proven one need not be a powerful warrior to conquer the Evil Queen. I want to thank you for saving my kingdom and reuniting my family."

Overcome with emotion, Cassy dropped to her knees and cried. She knew the danger was over, but for some reason, she could not seem to shake an uneasy feeling.

"I see you are tormented. What bothers you, child?" King Ashlym asked.

Cassy shook her head as she held out her hand. "I don't think the Blood Stone is working anymore. I think all of its magic is gone." She looked down at the Stone that now had a large crack in its center and had lost its deep red glow.

Cassy looked over at Roupert then at the Queen. "I know it was the Blood Key that brought me here, but now that Alona's curse and your spell are broken, it's no longer a key, right?"

"You are correct. It has returned to being the Blood Stone. Why do you ask?" Queen Privlana said.

Cassy lowered her head, afraid of the answer to come. "If it's no longer a key, then how are Aaron and I supposed to return home?"

King Ashlym tried his best not to laugh, "You do not fully understand the Power of the Dragon yet, do you?"

Cassy looked up at him and shook her head.

"You need not worry about how you will return home. You, as the Champion will always have the Power of the Dragon inside of you. You have shown great courage and defeated the Evil Queen Alona. Before you return to your home, let us celebrate with a grand feast. Today is a joyous day. Let us spend time together in celebration before you return to your realm," King Ashlym laughed heartily.

Chapter 23

Cassy's mind raced from the activities of the day. Roupert had taken her to the tower to retrieve the remainder of the Dragon clan, who had spent the many years of Alona's rule trapped as stone.

"I didn't realize there were so many of them," Cassy laughed as each took their turn greeting her and showering her with praise and well wishes.

"You are quite famous among the subjects of Walandra," Roupert laughed. Suddenly a young dragon transformed into the human form of a little girl, who ran up to Cassy and hugged her while giggling with tears of joy.

"Thank you for saving us," the little girl said while hugging Cassy tightly. "I did not like being trapped in stone for all that time."

Cassy looked up at Roupert with tears in her eyes. "I had no idea they would know what was happening to them. How terrible," she touched the little girl on the cheek, making her giggle even more.

"Come, we must hurry. We would not want to miss the feast," Roupert chuckled when the Dragons all transformed into their human forms and rushed to the stairway, which led down to the great hall.

Once Cassy and Roupert entered the Great Hall, Aaron ran up to Cassy and threw his arms around her neck.

"Hey, there, Sis, I sure am glad to see you. You're not going to believe this, but the Lillients showed me how to fly. I flew here from their castle far-off to the east. Man, I heard you beat that evil Alona and sent her packing."

Cassy held onto Aaron tightly, with joy filling her heart. "I'm glad to see you, too. You bet I did. You don't think I let some Evil Queen get the best of me, do you?" Cassy winked then laughed when Aaron shrugged his shoulders.

Cassy looked around the Great Hall. "Where are the Lillients? I'd like to thank them for taking such good care of you."

"They said something about needing to check on Frair. I hear he's no longer a small dragon and that he killed Alona. That is so cool," Aaron clapped his hands together joyously.

"Yeah, you wouldn't recognize him at all now," Cassy grinned.

A young maiden walked up to Cassy and held out her hand. "Please come with me, Cassandra, our Champion. The Queen has requested you dress for dinner. She said you must surely want to wash and change your clothes after such a grueling day. As for you, Sir Aaron, the Queen, would like you to go with Cameron. He will help you prepare for dinner."

Cassy and Aaron looked at each other, wondering how to respond.

Roupert walked up to them and rested his hand on Aaron's shoulder with a broad grin on his face. "Do not argue with orders from the Queen. Go with these servants, and they will help you prepare for dinner. I'll see you back here once you're done."

Realizing there was no sense in arguing, Cassy and Aaron followed the two servants out of the Hall and down a long hallway to the private chambers.

***

Cassy followed the servant girl through the large wooden door into a massive bedchamber. She looked around the room and was amazed at how beautifully it was decorated.

"Please remove your clothes and put them in the basket. I will see they are cleaned and returned to you after the feast."

The handmaiden walked over to a large tub sitting in the back of the room by a privacy screen. "You may undress behind there, and I will return with your dining clothes. The water is hot, and your soap and towel for drying are by the bath. If you need anything, please do not hesitate to ask. Once you have finished bathing, I will return to help you dress."

Cassy stepped behind the privacy screen and took off her clothes then put them in the basket. The handmaiden grabbed the basket with Cassy's dirty clothes and left the room. "Enjoy your bath, and I will return soon."

Cassy was at a loss for what to say, so she merely nodded and smiled. Once she was alone, she slipped into the warm bath.

As Cassy relaxed in the warm water, she thought back to the events of the past few days. No one would ever believe what she had done. To be honest, she was not sure if she understood it herself.

"Who would ever believe I was possessed by a Dragon and fought an Evil Queen using magic?" Cassy chuckled to herself.

She knew her life would never be the same after she returned home. How does someone experience everything she did and not be a changed person?

"Miss, it is nearly time to join everyone in the Great Hall," the handmaiden said as she walked back into the room carrying an elegant gown.

"Okay, I'm getting out." Cassy stood and reached for the towel. She would have enjoyed more time relaxing in the enticing water, but the serious look on the handmaiden's face let her know there was no time to waste.

"Please come over here. I laid your undergarments on the bed earlier, and I hope you find this gown pleasing. The Queen thought the color would bring out the beautiful color in your eyes," the handmaiden blushed at seeing the surprised look on Cassy's face.

"Ah, thank you. It's quite beautiful."

Once Cassy was dressed, the handmaiden had her sit so she could do her hair. "You have lovely hair, Miss Cassandra. I do hope you like what I do for you."

"I've never had anyone do my hair other than my mom," Cassy felt sadness tug at her heart.

The handmaiden smiled, "Your mother is a lucky woman to have such a brave daughter. To have been victorious over the Evil Queen is a miraculous thing. The subjects of the kingdom will eternally be in your debt."

"You don't owe me anything. I was just doing what I needed to do."

"No, you put the needs of others before those of your own. The children of Walandra will hear the tale of the young maiden from a faraway realm who saved us from the Evil Queen by casting her into the Land of the Shadows. They will sing praises to your name and rejoice in the freedom you restored."

Taken aback by the excitement in the handmaiden's eyes, Cassy's cheeks flushed a soft shade of red. "Thank you, that means a lot to me."

The handmaiden stepped away from Cassy and smiled. "There, you are ready. You are as beautiful as a Royal Princess, come, look." She took Cassy by the hand and led her over to the large mirror in the corner of the room.

Cassy's breath caught in her throat at the vision looking back at her in the mirror. She raised her hand to her mouth, "Oh, my, is that me?"

"Yes, you truly are a vision of beauty," the handmaiden nodded.

Cassy stared at the image looking back at her in the mirror. She noticed the dress was made of a shimmering amber cloth with a pearl-colored sash wrapped tightly around her waist. Cassy leaned in closer and saw the small jewels, each carefully sewn on the bodice of the dress, reflecting the flickering torches which hung along the walls of the room. Next, she realized how her hair was in a twisted knot on her head, with delicate wisps gently teasing her shoulders. Then atop her head, sat a small crown made of vibrant flowers.

"Thank you," Cassy said, unable to turn away from the image in the mirror.

"You are welcome. I'm sure Prince Frair will be pleased," the handmaiden winked.

Cassy glanced over at her, not understanding why she would say such a thing. "Ah, I don't understand. Frair and I are only friends and nothing more."

"As you say," the handmaiden giggled. "Come, we do not want you to be late for the feast."

***

A loud trumpet sounded, letting everyone know to sit at the Grand Table, as it was time for the Royal Family to enter the hall.

"Come; sit here," one of the service staff said, as he led Cassy and Aaron toward two elegant chairs near the head of the table.

Once they had taken their place, Cassy looked at Aaron and smiled. "You look so handsome. I never realized how much you look like Dad."

Aaron sat up straight, holding his chin high. "Roupert told me a Palace Guard is a Man of Honor and must act accordingly. I will watch over you, Fair Maiden, and keep you safe. One as lovely as you would surely be a prize for the evil forces," Aaron grinned playfully.

"Thank you fine, Sir, I am forever grateful to have such a brave Palace Guard protecting me." Cassy lowered her head with mock gratitude.

At hearing the murmurings of the others in the Grand Hall, Cassy and Aaron turned toward the large hallway where a man stood. He then announced in a loud and clear voice, "All behold, the Royal Family has returned. Let us all give praises for King Ashlym, Queen Privlana, and Prince Frair!"

Cassy turned, expecting to see the three fierce Dragons enter the Grand Hall, but instead three humans walked to the head of the table, causing her to gasp with surprise. She was amazed at how striking they were dressed in their elegant clothing. King Ashlym was tall and well-muscled with thick, wavy hair, and his eyes were the color of emeralds with flames swirling around in them.

He's quite a handsome man, Cassy had thought to herself.

She then glanced over to Queen Privlana, and Cassy marveled how much more beautiful she was now. Her dark auburn colored hair shimmered under the torch lights and the stunning green velvet gown she wore, only highlighted her beautiful green eyes, which now glistened with joy.

As Cassy focused her attention on the King and Queen, she did not notice the young man who had walked up from behind and stood beside her.

"My loyal subjects, I cannot begin to tell you how pleased we are to be back among you. It has been far too many years, but I believe our Kingdom will once again enjoy the prosperity it once knew. I am pleased to be reunited with our loving Queen and the Royal Prince. It is all because of the courage of our Champion, Cassandra," he smiled as he waved his hand toward Cassy, this bringing loud cheers from those gathered in the hall.

"Sit, my friends, and let us enjoy this feast prepared for us," King Ashlym said with a loud booming voice.

Once the King and Queen had sat in their chairs, Cassy felt someone sit next to her. She turned and found herself looking into familiar green eyes.

"Hello Cassy, it's good to see you again," Frair said with a broad smile on his face.

"Frair, is that you? You look...ah, so different," she struggled to find her words.

"As do you, you are quite beautiful tonight," Frair said as he took her hand in his.

Cassy felt her cheeks grow warm at his touch. "You are handsome as well."

"Thank you. I never knew I could transform into a human form. I wish I would have known earlier so I could have slept in the hut instead of outside for all those years," Frair grinned when he saw the surprised look appear on her face.

"But I understand why Roupert never told me, and I hold no ill will toward him."

Cassy found herself transfixed, unable to look away from Frair. In the short time they had known each other she had never felt the way she did now. The swirl of emotions, stirring up from deep inside of her confused her, so she forced herself to look away when the server set a plate of food in front of her.

"Thank you, that looks delicious," she said, glad to have the distraction.

Aaron leaned forward and looked at Frair. "I hope you don't mind, but I miss you as a Dragon. You were so cool with your wings and claws."

"Do not worry, Aaron. I can transform into the Dragon at any time. Maybe before you return to your realm, I will take you on a flight now that I'm big enough," Frair smiled when he saw the excited smile appear on Aaron's face.

"Let us eat before our food gets cold." Frair released Cassy's hand then turned to face his plate.

Cassy reached for her fork and wondered why she missed the touch of his hand so much as she took a bite of the roasted meat.

***

The time spent eating her meal was awkward for Cassy. She tried to keep her attention focused on her food, but she found herself glancing over at Frair. When they had first met, she had felt drawn to him, but she had believed it was because she had never met a Dragon before.

Yet, after seeing him in his human form, there was more to her feelings for him. Something she could not explain. She had had a crush on a boy before, but this was different. This was something tugging at her from deep within her soul.

She was absentmindedly pushing her peas around her plate when Frair spoke, "Are you feeling well? You seem distracted."

"I'm fine; I just had something on my mind, that's all." She scooped up some of the peas and put them in her mouth, hoping to ease the tense feelings churning inside of her.

Frair laughed softly as he took her hand in his again. "I can't explain it either, but I feel it too. We will speak once everyone is finished eating. Father has ordered a Ball in celebration of our return, and he wants to honor you. I hope you will honor me by dancing with me."

Cassy felt his eyes look into hers with such intensity she was convinced he had seen into her heart and saw the feelings tucked safely away for him there.

"I would love to dance with you, Frair." She pulled her hand away and continued to eat her meal, doing her best not to make eye contact with him.

Roupert sat across the table from Cassy, Frair, and Aaron during dinner. He had watched the stolen glances between Cassy and Frair, remembering the time he had spent with Abigail. How he longed to see her face again now that the kingdom was safe, but he knew it would never be.

At seeing the others leave the Grand Hall, Aaron jumped to his feet. "Come on, you two. I've never been to a dance before."

Frair stood and offered his hand to Cassy, who placed her hand on his. "Thank you, Frair."

"It is my honor to escort the most beautiful maiden to the Ball," Frair said, hoping to impress her with his gallantry.

Aaron looked at the two of them and rolled his eyes. "What the heck is wrong with you two? If I didn't know better, I'd think you liked each other…"

Cassy turned toward Aaron and gave him a threatening glare. "Quiet, I don't want to hear any of your foolishness tonight. Do you understand me?"

Aaron had seen that look in her eyes before, and he knew not to push her any further. "Sure, I'm sorry. I'm just excited, that's all."

Aaron looked up at Frair, who smiled, letting him know he had done nothing wrong. "Come; let us go to the ball. Aaron, I would like to introduce you to my cousin, Dalaina. She is the same age, so I know you both will become great friends. Besides, she is an excellent dancer from what I understand, and since this is your first time to attend a ball, she will be a great help to you."

Aaron looked at Cassy, unsure of what to say. While he was excited to be going to the dance, he was nervous he would appear a fool to Frair's cousin. "Are you sure she'd want to dance with me? I've never done any of that fancy stuff people do at a ball."

Frair rested his hand on Aaron's shoulder. "I promise by the Power of the Dragon you will dance with poise and grace tonight. All those at the ball will speak in the days ahead of how Aaron, the brother of our Champion danced with the beautiful Dalaina.

Cassy watched as Frair's hand began to glow softly as it rested on Aaron's shoulder. Then when he removed his hand, she suddenly noticed a look of confidence appear on Aaron's face.

"Bring it on. I'm ready to rock her world," Aaron said with a broad grin on his face as he turned and followed the others to the Ball Room.

Once Cassy and Frair were alone, she turned to look at him. "You used magic on him, didn't you? You used magic so he'd know how to dance."

Frair looked into her eyes and smiled. "No, I only gave him the confidence to try. He was so scared that he was destroying any chance of having fun. I only removed his doubt. The rest is up to him."

"Has anyone told you today how wonderful you are?" Cassy reached up and gently kissed his cheek.

"My mother did, but I must say I enjoy it much more from you. Come; let us join the others." Frair took her by the hand and led her toward the Ball Room.

Chapter 24

Cassy had never seen anything so grand in her life. Candelabras lined the walls with candles casting an elegant mood over the dance floor. She felt like a Princess in a Fairytale, and she wondered if she was dreaming.

"Come with me," Frair whispered as she held onto his arm.

Frair led Cassy to the large table where the King and Queen sat with other people who Cassy assumed were other members of the Royal Family. Frair walked to the four empty chairs next to the King and Queen.

"Please sit here. I will be right back." Frair held the chair for Cassy as she sat, then he pointed to a chair, letting Aaron know to wait for him there.

Once Frair disappeared into the gathered crowd, Aaron leaned over to Cassy. "It looks like something is going on between you two. At first, I wasn't sure about it, but now it makes sense. I know we're supposed to go home soon, but I believe somehow the two of you will find each other again."

Cassy looked into Aaron's eyes and saw the love they shared as brother and sister looking back at her. "How did you grow up so quickly?"

"I don't know. It must have something to do with hanging out with the Lillients," Aaron snickered when he saw the surprised look on Cassy's face.

"You know, I was hoping I'd get to see them again before we leave. I'd like to thank them for keeping me safe while you went after Alona, even though I still think I could have been some help."

"I'm sure you would have been. I'd like to thank them as well, and I'd like to thank Keira, the Milif, for all of her help as well. I know I wouldn't have been able to do everything I did without her help."

Aaron felt a hand rest on his shoulder, and when he turned to see who it was, he found himself lost in the most beautiful pair of green eyes he had ever seen. He quickly jumped to his feet with his heart pounding wildly in his chest.

"Aaron, I would like to introduce my lovely cousin, Dalaina. She has graciously agreed to be your dance partner this evening." Frair glanced down at Cassy and gave her a playful wink.

Aaron's mind spun wildly. What was he expected to do when meeting Royalty? Was he supposed to bow? Was he supposed to take her hand?

Oh no, what do I do? The words screamed in his mind.

"I am honored to spend the evening with such a dashing young man, Aaron," Dalaina smiled as she offered him her hand.

Aaron looked at Dalaina and smiled nervously as he took the offered hand. He paused a moment, unsure of what to do next when Frair pulled her seat back, allowing her to sit.

"Thank you, Frair," Dalaina held her gaze on Aaron, who still had her hand in his. "You may let go of my hand now, Aaron."

Realizing how foolish he must look, Aaron released her hand then sat in the chair next to her without saying a word.

As Frair sat in the chair next to Cassy, a large man sitting next to the orchestra stood and made an announcement. "Tonight, is a joyous time for the Kingdom of Walandra and its people. In honor of the return of the Royal Family, we shall begin with a waltz from the King and Queen."

Everyone in the room turned and watched as the King and Queen stood and walked to the center of the dance floor. Once in place, the music started, and the King and Queen began to dance to a hauntingly beautiful tune. Cassy marveled at how they seemed to float across the dance floor as the orchestra played. Suddenly, the King motioned to Frair to join them on the dance floor.

"Shall we?" Frair stood and offered his arm.

Without thinking, Cassy stood and wrapped her arm around his. She felt as though she were caught up in a dream as she walked with him to the dance floor. He then turned to face her with his gaze burning into hers, making her feel as though at any moment flames would consume her. She had no idea what she was doing when she rested one hand on his shoulder. Then she gasped when he placed his hand on her waist, and with the other, he held her free hand in his.

"I don't know how to dance like this," Cassy whispered.

"Neither do I, but I have faith in the Power of the Dragon. I believe we will do fine," Frair smiled as they began to gracefully dance across the floor.

Cassy held her eyes closed until she heard Frair whisper in her ear. "Open your eyes, my dear Cassandra. I want you to remember this night for the rest of your life."

Cassy slowly opened her eyes, and to her amazement, she was floating across the dance floor, doing a proper waltz to the hauntingly beautiful music.

"I can't believe I'm doing this," she giggled. "My sister, Melissa, would never believe it."

"Hey, Sis, do you think Mom and Dad would believe I can do this?" Aaron chuckled as he and Dalaina twirled past her and Frair.

"Wow, look at you. I didn't know you could dance like that," Cassy said with pride.

"It wasn't all me, Frair did it," Aaron grinned playfully as he and Dalaina danced off to the other side of the room.

Cassy looked up at Frair, enjoying the smile on Aaron's face."

"Thank you for helping him, but I have a question. When did you bestow a touch of the Dragon on me? I've never danced this way before, either."

Frair leaned down and placed his cheek against hers as he whispered in her ear. "I did not need to bestow the Power of the Dragon on you because you already have it within you. You see, just because you no longer wear the sacred Breast Plate and Blood Key does not mean the Power of the Dragon removed itself from you. What you don't understand is it will be with you for the rest of your life. It doesn't matter if you are in Walandra or in your realm. You are now and forever part of the Dragon."

Cassy pulled away, unsure if she had heard him correctly. "Are you saying I still have the same powers I did when I was on my quest to vanquish Alona? How is that possible? The curse is broken, and your father returned from the Land of Shadows. You must be wrong. I'm just back to being the same old Cassy I was before I came here."

Frair's expression transformed into one of sadness. "I thought you felt the power still inside of you as I feel it in you. That is what draws us to each other."

Cassy shook her head, trying to understand the depth of his words. "I can't be drawn to you in that way. I'm going to turn seventeen-years-old next week. I'll be returning to High School in the fall, and if I keep my grades up, Mom and Dad are planning to buy me a car. I'm not ready for what you offer. I'm still a kid. Aaron and I need to return to our family. We can't stay here, I'm sorry," tears flowed down her cheeks as she realized what her words meant.

Saddened by her decision, Frair also understood the desire to be with one's family.

After learning he had a family, the last thing he could do was to request Cassy to leave hers.

"Then, let us enjoy this night of dance and merriment before you return to your realm." Frair pulled her back into his arms then they danced across the floor as though floating on air.

Roupert sat in the corner next to the orchestra, watching the dancers as they enjoyed the festivities.

He could not help but wonder what would happen now that Cassy had restored the King and Queen to the throne. He knew King Ashlym would want him to return as the head of the Palace Guard.

Roupert had to admit there was a part of him that had longed for that day, but he also had to admit he would miss his little hut in the woods. He would also miss his time with the little dragon that had brought so much joy to his life. Now that they had returned to the castle, he wondered how his relationship with Frair would be from this time forward.

"Are you reminiscing about times long gone? A small voice filled his mind.

"Keira, is that you?" Roupert turned his head looking for the tiny Milif when he noticed her sitting on the shoulder of one of the violinists in the orchestra.

"It is rather noisy in here. Let us step out on the balcony for a short talk," Keira said, and then in a flash of light, she was gone.

Roupert had to laugh when the violinist nearly jumped out of his chair from fright when Keira vanished. Once he realized the poor man was okay, he stood and walked toward the door leading outside.

"I'm over by the fountain," Keira's voice sounded in Roupert's mind.

"Okay, I'm coming," he said aloud, feeling the fool should anyone has heard him.

Once he was at the fountain, he sat on the stone bench and waited.

"Thank you for meeting with me, Roupert. I have important news for you."

Roupert leaned back and crossed his arms over his chest. "Okay, what was so important that you had to take me away from the festivities?"

"It is about Abigail."

Roupert's breath caught in his throat at the mention of her name. "What of Abigail? Why do you speak of her now?"

Keira could sense the sadness in Roupert's heart. "I know your feelings for Abigail. They burn with the same intensity today, as they did all those years ago."

Roupert shook his head, unwilling to have his heart reminded of the pain he endured the day the Blood Key returned her to her realm. "Please, that is one subject I would prefer not to discuss."

"I understand the pain you feel at losing her, but I want you to know the day comes when the pain you feel will disappear forever."

Roupert shook his head, unsure if he had heard her correctly. "I don't understand. How is that even possible? We no longer need a Champion, and with the Queen's spell is broken, the Blood Stone is no longer a key. Soon Cassy and Aaron will return to their realm, so any need for magic between our worlds will no longer exist."

"Please, Roupert, I wish I could say more, but I am forbidden. Just know should things transpire as expected, you will see your beloved Abigail again. You need to send forth your desire to see her again and let her know eternal happiness awaits her with you in Walandra. For this to happen, it will take the strongest magic in all the realms even more powerful than that of the Dragon - The Power of Love. Of course, please don't tell King Ashlym what I said," Keira laughed playfully.

Is it so? Could Abigail return to him? Roupert felt his heart come alive and fill with hope. "I want that more than anything, Keira. My heart has been empty without her."

"Then once Cassy and Aaron return to their realm, you must put forth the love you have for Abigail so she will feel it across the vast distance between our realms. For that is the only way to summon her back to you."

Is it true? Can I actually be reunited with my beloved Abigail? The words caused his heart to leap with hope.

"Yes, it is true, my dear friend. The time comes for Abigail to leave this life in her realm. She is alone, and her heart aches for her one true love. If you want to save her from death, you need to let her know she is wanted here with you."

Roupert turned and looked at Keira, his eyes suddenly filled with tears. "What do you mean by saving her from death? Is she in danger? Is someone trying to harm her?"

Keira flew closer to Roupert. She reached out and gently touched him on the cheek. "No, my dear friend, in her realm she has grown to be an old woman who has come to the end of her life. Soon she will die and be gone forever, so if you want to spare her the journey of death, you will need to reach out to her and summon her here to be with you. Do not doubt your love for her, Roupert. She will come to you when the time is right. All you need to do is ask, but you must not tell Cassandra or her brother. They must not know of this as it would affect their decisions for their own life paths."

Roupert nodded. "I understand, Keira. Thank you for telling me about this. My heart has been empty for so many years, and now that Frair has returned to his parents I had feared what my purpose would be."

He exhaled, feeling the agony, he had felt for all these long years gone from his heart. "I best return to the festivities before someone realizes I'm gone."

Roupert bowed to Keira. She, in turn, returned the bow out of respect.

"Roupert, I have something else important I must do before the morning. We will see each other again, my friend."

Before Roupert could say more, she was gone in a flash of light.

"Goodbye, my little friend. Thank you for the joyous news of my beloved, Abigail." With a new lightness in his heart, Roupert returned to the festivities and sat at the table with his friends.

"You look pleased with yourself," Frair teased.

"As do you, young Prince," Roupert winked when he noticed he and Cassy were holding hands.

Realizing what Roupert meant, Frair lifted Cassy's hand and gently kissed it. "Yes, I am, and I fully plan to enjoy myself for as long as our time together lasts."

Roupert noticed the mixture of love and sadness in Cassy's eyes, and he felt his heartbreak at knowing the pain of loss she and Frair would endure once she returned to her realm. "Yes, enjoy each precious moment, for you never know when you will have such joy in your hearts again."

The orchestra began to play another song. "May I have this dance?" Frair stood and held out his hand for Cassy.

"Yes, I would love to dance with you," she said in a soft voice as he led her out on the dance floor.

Roupert watched as Frair and Cassy danced to the soothing music, and he wondered what their futures held for them. He could see the love burning in Frair's eyes for Cassy, and he knew once a Dragon fell in love that love lasted forever.

"So much for a Dragon's love being the only one to last for all time. My love for Abigail has endured the pain-filled years as well," he silently said to himself, as he softly laughed at how life sometimes will play cruel tricks on one's heart.

As the music played, Roupert watched each couple dance across the floor. He then breathed a sigh of relief at knowing the dangers the Kingdom had faced all those long years were finally behind them.

Chapter 25

Everyone had danced late into the night, so Cassy agreed she and Aaron would return home in the morning at the King's request.

As she lay on her bed, she thought back to the wonderful evening, and no matter how much Cassy did not want to admit it, she was in love with Frair.

"How is that even possible? I've only known him a few days, and most of that time, he was a young, silly Dragon."

She closed her eyes, and his face appeared in her mind. She had never known anyone as handsome as Frair. His eyes seemed to hold her captive. She found herself lost in the deep, shimmering emerald green with the swirling flames that appeared to dance on their own. His hair was dark and wavy with soft, loose curls teasing his neck and shoulders. As they danced across the floor, she found herself gently twirling his hair with her fingers of the hand resting on his shoulder.

At one point, he had realized what she was doing and merely smiled as they continued to dance.

"Stop thinking that way. You're going home tomorrow, and you will never see him again. Besides, he's a Prince, in line for the throne.

You're not Princess material, let alone someone who could ever be a Queen. Just let this go and get some sleep," she scolded herself for thinking such foolish thoughts.

As she struggled to fall asleep, Cassy heard a soft voice in her mind. "Cassandra, we need to talk."

"Who's here?" Cassy sat up on the bed and looked around the room. She suddenly noticed a small ball of light floating across the room toward the bed.

"Keira, is that you?"

"Hello, Cassandra. It is good to see you again," Keira flew up to the bed then sat on the pillow next to Cassy.

Cassy looked down at Keira and marveled at how lovely she was with the shimmering light surrounding her. "It's good to see you too, Keira. What brings you here tonight?"

"I have been here the entire evening, watching over the festivities. I see you and Frair had an enjoyable time," she winked playfully.

Cassy felt her cheeks warm at the idea of Keira watching her with Frair. "Yes, he was quite a surprise."

"I'm sure he was. It was a joy to see the Prince as he was meant to be. He will be a great King someday "

"I'm sure he will," Cassy said with a hint of sadness in her voice.

Keira saw the sorrow in Cassy's eyes, and she understood her torn feelings as she faced the decision to return to her own realm. Moreover,

Keira knew it would only be temporary as fate had a different future planned for Cassandra, the Champion of Walandra.

"I know you will be returning to your realm tomorrow, and I have something important for you to do once you are there," Keira saw the surprised look on Cassy's face and smiled.

"Hold out your hand, sweet child."

Cassy did as instructed, and in a swirling flash of red light, she saw the Blood Stone lying in the palm of her hand. "I don't understand. I thought the Blood Stone was returned to its safe place."

"That is what the King and Queen believe, but it has another important task to perform."

Cassy tipped her head to the side, unsure if she understood why Keira would give her the Blood Stone.

"You will take the Blood Stone with you to your realm tomorrow, and once there, you will give it to Abigail."

"You want me to give it to my great-grandmother. Why? Won't the book already be there in her library?"

Keira began to laugh. "No, you silly child; the book is no longer in Abigail's library. It came with you to Walandra. You wore it during your quest."

Cassy shook her head, trying to understand. "Are you saying the sacred Breast Plate was actually the book? I know that's what was said, but I never actually believed it to be true."

"Yes, it was true. You see, when Abigail came to Walandra, she was unable to break the curse. Therefore, when Alona was about to take her life, the Blood Key returned itself, the sacred Breast Plate, and Abigail to your realm."

"I don't understand. If she loved Roupert and he loved her, why didn't she return?"

Keira exhaled before speaking again. "She could not return because she forgot about Walandra and everyone she met here. Once she had returned to your realm, she learned of her Grandfather's death, so in her grief, she forgot all about her time here."

"How sad, and that explains the look of sadness in her eyes." Cassy could not imagine what it would be like to lose one of her parents.

"It was as it was meant to be. Had Abigail not returned to your realm, you never would have been born. I never understood until you came to us, but that was the plan from the beginning."

"But I still don't understand. Why do you want me to give her the Blood Stone?" Cassy looked down at the stone, now glowing in her hand.

"It is not necessary you understand at this time. Abigail will know what to do with it when the time comes. I leave it with you, so please guard it well. There are still forces in this realm that would like to have its powers. I will cast a protection spell to surround you until you return to your realm, but please tell no one you possess the stone. Do you understand?"

Cassy nodded her head as she held the Blood Stone in her hand.

"I see they have provided you with a nightgown," Keira grinned.

"Yes, and it's quite comfortable," Cassy rubbed her hand on the soft fabric.

"Well, I will take my leave of you, Cassandra. I am thankful for everything you have done for the Kingdom of Walandra. Your courage and determination are a tribute to the brave soul you are, as well as the woman you will become in your life."

"Thank you, Keira. It has been an honor, knowing you."

Keira took flight and then bowed. "Goodbye, our brave Champion; until we meet again."

Before Cassy could respond, Keira disappeared in a bright flash of light.

After Keira had vanished, Cassy dropped down on her pillow, mulling over their conversation. She held out the Blood Stone and looked at it again.

"So, I'm to give this to my great-grandmother, and she will know what to do when the time is right. If she doesn't remember Walandra and everything she did here, that doesn't make any sense."

Realizing there was no point in worrying, she held the Blood Stone firmly against her chest. She then closed her eyes, and after a few restless minutes, Cassy finally slipped off into a dream-filled slumber filled with happy memories of her evening with Frair.

***

The sun rose above the mountains and woke the subjects of Walandra for their first full day of freedom from the Evil Queen Alona. Everyone scurried about doing their chores with a renewed sense of joy in their hearts. The birds' songs seemed to carry a cheerful melody, the flowers appeared to smell sweeter, and the rest of the Kingdom seemed caught up in a new feeling of tranquility.

Cassy stirred from her slumber at the sound of the handmaiden entering the room.

"Good morning, I hope you slept well?" The handmaiden entered the room, carrying a basket with Cassy's freshly washed clothes.

Cassy sat up in the bed, yawning and stretching. "Yes, as a matter of fact, I slept quite well."

"Good. I was sent to bring you to eat breakfast with the Royal family. The Queen thought you should eat before you return to your realm. Besides, I believe the King has something he wishes to give you."

The handmaiden removed the clothes from the basket and laid them on the bed next to Cassy.

"Your clothes are washed for you. I hope you find them satisfactory."

"Thank you, they're fine," Cassy grinned as she got out of the bed.

"Splendid, I will leave you for now." The handmaiden turned and walked toward the door.

"Oh, well, let's not leave them waiting," Cassy smiled as she reached for her clothes.

"Please give me a moment to gather my things, and I'll join you in the hallway."

Once the handmaiden had left the room, Cassy quickly removed the nightgown. She laughed at how her pajamas and robe had magically transformed into the warrior clothing she had worn while on her quest. "I guess it was more of that Power of the Dragon stuff. I am going to miss those boots, though," Cassy laughed as she looked down at the slippers sitting on the floor next to her bed.

Cassy reached under the pillow on the bed and pulled out the Blood Stone then she picked up her robe and put it on. "Okay, let's put you in here for safekeeping," Cassy said aloud as she put the Blood Stone in one of the pockets of the robe. Once convinced she had everything, Cassy walked toward the door. Before opening the door, she turned and looked back at the beautiful room.

"It's a shame I'll never come back here again." She then reached for the door handle, opened the door, and joined the handmaiden in the hall.

***

When Cassy entered the room, she noticed Aaron was already seated at the table with Frair. They appeared to be eating a massive platter of pancakes.

"Good morning, it's about time you woke up. Heck, Frair already took me for a morning flight," Aaron said with a mouthful of the tasty treat.

Cassy walked over to the table and sat in the open chair between them. "He did? I bet you had a blast. I see now you're enjoying your breakfast," she laughed as he took another huge bite and crammed it into his mouth.

"Oh, man, that was the best time ever. I wish I were a Dragon. I was hoping to go again, but I know we're leaving soon."

Cassy looked at Frair and saw him smile. "Thank you for doing that."

"I enjoyed taking him. We had a good time," Frair responded.

Aaron took another large bite of his food as he rolled his eyes, "I don't know what this stuff is, but it's delicious. Mom needs the recipe."

"Your brother has a healthy appetite," Frair chuckled as he watched Aaron take another bite.

"Yeah, Dad always said he'd probably eat us if we ever ran out of food." Cassy then laughed when she saw the surprised expression appear on Frair's face.

"You are joking, correct? While I know he loves to eat, I do not believe he would try to eat you, or your family."

Cassy could not help but laugh at the concerned look on Frair's face. "Yes, I'm only joking. It's just a figure of speech. Aaron would never eat us, at least, I hope not."

Aaron looked at Cassy and grinned. "I'd never eat you because I'd probably get a bad stomach ache, but Melissa might be tasty. With all those creams to keep her skin soft, she might be extra tender."

Frair broke out into raucous laughter at Aaron, not wanting to eat Cassy. "So, you say her twin sister is much more delicate. How interesting…"

Cassy glared at Aaron then at Frair. She did not understand why, but she was nervous at the idea of Melissa meeting Frair.

Aaron saw the look in her eyes and sensed her fear. "Hey, you wouldn't like Melissa, Frair. While she may look like Cassy, she isn't as cool. I promise you had it been Melissa facing the Evil Queen, your kingdom would have been screwed. No, Cassy is the brave one in the family, and I'm proud to be her brother."

Cassy looked at Aaron with both surprise and gratitude shining in her eyes. "Thank you, Aaron. I'm proud of you as well. This sure has been an adventure for us, hasn't it?"

Aaron nodded his head and then returned to eating his breakfast.

Frair raised his hand, summing one of the servers to bring Cassy's meal. Once they all had their meals, they ate in silence as they contemplated the events to come.

Chapter 26

Cassy leaned back in her chair and rubbed her overstuffed stomach. "Those were absolutely delicious. What were they called?"

Frair placed his fork on his plate and pushed it away from him. "They are called Templends. They are a favorite among my people. Roupert used to make them for me on special occasions. I only wish I would have stopped eating them two plates ago," Frair groaned.

"Speaking of Roupert, where is he this morning?" Cassy looked around the room, hoping to see him.

"He is meeting with my Father and the Castle Guards. They are discussing security issues for the Castle."

It had surprised Cassy why they would need special security for the Castle. "Why do they need to worry about security now? Alona's gone, so any danger you may face is gone, right?"

Frair reached over and took Cassy's hand in his. "Do not worry about such things. My Father is a mighty King, so anyone wanting to do us harm will not find victory here. It is just a routine meeting; that's all. Come; please join me for a walk in the garden. I would like to have some time alone before you return to your realm."

Frair stood then led Cassy outside to the garden just off the balcony where Roupert had spoken to Keira the night before.

As they strolled down the path leading to the large water fountain, Cassy could not help but feel sorrow at the thought of leaving Frair and Walandra behind. She knew it was foolish to feel this way, but something deep inside her did not want to leave. She glanced over at Frair and felt her heart quicken. Once at the fountain, they sat on the beautifully carved bench below a large tree.

Frair looked over at Cassy and swallowed, trying to gather his thoughts before he spoke. He knew she would be leaving soon, but he wanted her to know his feelings before she left him forever. "Cassy."

"Yes, Frair."

He turned so he could look into her eyes. "I know we are both young, and we have separate lives, but I wanted you to know how I feel about you before you go."

Cassy gazed deeply into his eyes and felt as though her heart would break into a million pieces. She wanted to respond, but the words evaded her lips.

Frair saw the emotions stirring in Cassy and felt overcome with his love for her. "As you know, once a Dragon surrenders his heart, and it is lost to them forever. I love you, Cassy, and even though we will live realms apart, you will always possess my heart."

He lifted her hand to his lips and kissed it gently.

Cassy could no longer hold back the tears escaping from the corners of her eyes. She wanted to throw herself into his arms and tell him she would stay with him, but she knew that was impossible. She had to take Aaron home and give her great-grandmother the Blood Stone, as she had promised Keira.

"Frair, I wish I could stay with you and live here forever, but I can't. I have to return to my family. I have obligations and things I need to do." She reached up and wiped the tears from her eyes, hoping she had convinced him.

He turned his head away, fighting the pain crushing his heart. "I understand obligations. I have many things my Father expects of me, as well. Learning the truth of who I am and having everything I believed my entire life turned upside down is quite unnerving. The only thing that has made it bearable is you. When we met that first day, I felt something come alive deep inside of me I could not explain. A powerful force awakened when I saw you standing there. I did not know what it was, but for some reason, I sensed we would be in each other's lives. I did not know how or why, but my heart told me you would always be special to me."

Cassy tipped her head to the side, surprised at his words. "But you never let on. I knew we were friends, but you never let on there was any more than friendship."

Frair chuckled, "It's because I did not understand it myself. I was under my Mother's spell in which not only was I trapped in the body of a young boy, but I had the emotions of one as well. It was not until the spell was broken, and I gained my Dragon powers and memories that I thoroughly understood the overpowering feelings I had for you."

Cassy shook her head and laughed softly. "In my realm, people often speak of love at first sight, but this isn't as simple as that, is it?"

Frair reached up and wiped the tears wetting her cheeks. "No, it is not. I know you care for me. I can see it in your eyes. The Power of the Dragon has joined our hearts, and I wanted you to know I will forever love you."

"Oh, Frair, it's so unfair," she cried out, throwing her arms around his neck. "I can't stay with you. I'm sorry."

Cassy held on to him, not wanting to let go. She knew their time together was coming to an end, and she would never see him again.

How can one love someone so deeply in such a short time? The words burned in her mind.

She pressed her cheek against his and whispered in his ear, "I love you too, and I will for the rest of my life."

Frair did not want this moment to end, but he knew the others would wonder where they had gone. Lifting her face to his, he pressed his lips to hers.

How can I go on without her by my side? An agonizing torment consumed his entire being.

Once their lips had parted, he gazed deeply into her tear-filled eyes. "I have something I want to give you as a symbol of my love."

Stepping back, he plucked a red rose from one of the nearby bushes. "Some legends say the red rose represents the heart of a Dragon. I give you this rose, as I have given you my heart."

Taking the rose, Cassy placed it to her lips. "I take your heart and give mine in return."

Both stood, caught up in this moment, neither wanting it to end. As they gazed deeply into each other's eyes, a gentle breeze carried the sounds of laughter from the celebration inside. Realizing they must rejoin the festivities, they turned and with clasped hands, walked back through the large doors.

***

"Ah, there you two are," Roupert laughed when he saw the flushed looks on their faces.

"I thought we were going to have to send out the Palace Guards to bring you back inside. The King and Queen have been waiting," Roupert winked playfully.

Frair and Cassy exchanged embarrassed glances then followed Roupert to the Great Hall.

"There they are. We were wondering when you two would join us," King Ashlym teased. "Please, come here."

Frair and Cassy walked to where the King and Queen were standing with several of the Royal family.

"Cassandra, please come stand by me," the King smiled as he waited for her.

She glanced over at Frair, not wanting to leave his side.

"Go on, the King awaits," Frair smiled as he released her hand.

Cassy walked over to the King and Queen with her heart pounding in her chest as she wondered what they wanted.

"Behold, our Champion, Cassandra. She came to us from another realm, summand by the Blood Key. Through the selfless acts of bravery, she bested the Evil Queen Alona and made it possible to banish her to the Land of Shadows for all eternity."

Cheers erupted from those gathered around. "Praises for our Champion, Cassandra!"

Cassy looked up at the King and noticed the broad smile on his face. He held up his hand to silence the crowd and then turned to Cassy. "We will forever be in your debt. The Queen and I wish to bestow a gift showing our appreciation for all you have done."

He turned and retrieved a necklace from a small jeweled box. "This amulet has special powers that will give you the ability to return to Walandra should your heart wish to return." He took the necklace and handed it to Frair.

Cassy turned her back to Frair, allowing him to put the necklace around her neck. Once it was in place, she lifted the amulet and looked at it.

"It looks like the Blood Stone, only smaller. Thank you, it's beautiful," she said in a near whisper.

She gently ran her fingertip across the face of the amulet, when a familiar sensation surged through her body. "It's you," she said with surprise in her voice as she whirled around and faced Frair.

"Father didn't want you to forget Walandra. He and Mother both hope someday you will return to us... to me," he looked into her eyes with hope burning in his heart.

Cassy knew what she wanted to say, but she also knew she must remain strong. "Thank you, King Ashlym; I will forever treasure your gift."

"You are quite welcome; nevertheless, my son has not told you everything the amulet will do. It will not only bring you back to us should you desire to return, but it will also return you and Aaron to your realm."

Cassy ran her fingertip over the face of the amulet again and felt the power trapped inside. "Thank you, I promise to guard it forever."

"We hope you are not going to leave without saying goodbye, Cassandra," Syrea said, as she and the other two Lillients appeared beside the King and Queen.

"I would also hope our special friend Aaron does not leave without saying goodbye," Arianna added.

"Yes, we would truly be sad," Brianna said as she flew up to Aaron and kissed his cheek, causing him to giggle.

"I'm so glad you came to say goodbye. I never would have been able to complete my task had it not been for your help," Cassy bowed to the Lillients with respect for their support during her difficult time against Alona.

"Yeah, I want to thank you for keeping me safe. You three are the best," Aaron bowed as well.

"It was our honor," the three said in unison.

"What about me? I came all this way to say goodbye. Have you forgotten me?" Othan grinned as he stepped forward.

"Othan; how wonderful to see you again. I want to thank you for your help and for giving me the nectar. It worked just as you promised." Cassy leaned down and hugged Othan then kissed him on the cheek.

Othan reached his hand up and touched his cheek. "I will forever treasure this kiss. Thank you, Cassandra."

Laughter broke out in the hall at the look of pure joy on Othan's face.

"Cassandra, I do believe you have done the impossible. You have made that old man smile," King Ashlym laughed uncontrollably.

Othan looked at Cassy and merely shrugged his shoulders, this bringing another round of laughter.

Once everyone had settled down, King Ashlym raised his hand and announced, "We have kept our friends for long enough. Cassandra, I want you and Aaron to know you both will be greatly missed. You have given us a gift that can never be adequately repaid, but I hope you will remember us and know you will forever be in our hearts."

He reached out and took Cassy in his arms and hugged her tightly. Once he was done, the Queen embraced both Cassy and Aaron.

The King turned to Aaron and held out his hand. "I did not know what gift a young man from your realm would enjoy, so I asked my son what he thought you might like. He informed me you are quite taken with anything of the Dragon. Maybe this will bring you joy and help you not to forget us."

King Ashlym handed Aaron an object wrapped in cloth. "Go ahead and open it."

Aaron quickly unwrapped the object, and once he realized what it was, he shouted with joy. "This is so cool! It's a Dragon's scale!" Aaron smiled as he held it up for Cassy to see.

"That is not just any scale. That is the scale of a King," Frair laughed when he saw the look of disbelief appear on Aaron's face.

"Really? Thank you, your Majesty," Aaron bowed before King Ashlym.

"It was the least I could do for the brave brother of our Champion," King Ashlym smiled tenderly. "Still, there is something you must remember. If you were to try to show it to anyone other than Cassandra, it would return to Walandra. No one must ever know you have been here. Not your friends, not even your parents. I am sorry, but that is how it must be."

"I understand, and I promise to obey the rules. Thank you again."

"Wonderful, then all is done. It is time for you two to return to your realm."

"Not until I get to say goodbye," Roupert said as he stepped forward, taking Cassy in his arms and hugging her tightly. "Thank you for everything you have done. I will never forget you."

Cassy rested her head against his chest. "I'll never forget you either, Roupert. Thank you for having faith in me. I never could have done it without you."

"Hey, what about me?" Aaron crossed his arms in protest.

Roupert released Cassy, then grabbed Aaron and pulled him close, hugging him tightly. "I could never forget you, my brave warrior."

"Hey, you're crushing me," Aaron laughed as he struggled to free himself from Roupert's embrace.

Once he had freed himself, Cassy looked at Aaron. "Are you ready to go home?"

"I guess so," he said with sadness in his voice.

Cassy felt Frair take her by the hand, and when she turned to face him, she saw tears in his eyes.

"I do not want you to leave," he pleaded.

"I know, but I must; I'm sorry."

"May I kiss you one more time before you go?" The look in his eyes showed her the deep sorrow he was feeling.

"Yes," she whispered.

Cassy found herself lost in a whirlwind of emotions when he gently pressed his lips to hers.

Time stood still as they shared the kiss, they both knew would be their last. Cassy felt her resolve begin to waver, so she stepped back, ending the dream of love unfulfilled.

"Okay, we're ready," she said, keeping her eyes transfixed on Frair.

Cassy reached for the amulet and held it in her hand. She glanced over at the King and Queen, who both nodded, offering their encouragement. She then reached for Aaron's hand and pulled him close to her.

Her heart was screaming in pain, as she held the amulet. Suddenly, a strange fog seemed to appear in the room, hiding everyone from her sight.

"What's going on?" she said, but no one responded.

"Do not fear, Cassandra. It is I, Keira."

"Keira? Have you come to say goodbye? If so, why all the mystery?"

Keira appeared in front of Cassy, with a look of seriousness on her face. "I have come to tell you something of great importance. It is about the amulet the King gave you."

"Okay, what else do I need to know other than it will take me home and bring me back here should I decide I want to return?"

"Do you remember the intense emotions you felt when you held it for the first time?"

"Yes, I felt Frair. It was as if our hearts had become one and not in the, I love him sort of way, but something deeper, something, almost spiritual. Am I making any sense?"

"Yes, and I know the reason you felt that way. You see, the King has no idea what Frair did, and it must stay that way."

"I don't understand. What did Frair do?" Cassy suddenly felt fear well up inside of her.

"You are aware of how, when a Dragon falls in love, they will love that one person for all time, correct?"

Cassy nodded, letting Keira know she understood.

"Frair has freely given you his heart, Cassandra. When the Blood Key chose you, it opened a doorway between your hearts. You may never fully understand what that means, but you have a great future ahead of you. Frair realized that fact and wanted to ensure you would be able to fulfill your destiny. He knows there will be forces who will want to prevent you from doing what you are meant to do. He also knew there was only one way he could give you the power you would need."

Cassy's eyes grew wide with fear. "Please don't tell me..."

Keira nodded her head, "I'm afraid he did. It was out of his love for you. The amulet you hold in your hand contains a drop of Frair's blood, so as long as you wear it, your hearts shall be as one. You will share his power to protect yourself from any who would do you harm. In spite of this, be warned. Should you lose the amulet, you will curse Frair to the Land of Shadows forever. Do you understand?"

Cassy looked at Keira through tear-filled eyes and merely nodded.

"Good. You still have the Blood Stone to give Abigail, correct?"

"Yes, it's in my pocket," Cassy reached into the pocket on her robe and pulled out the Blood Stone then held it up.

"Remember to give it to Abigail as soon as you return."

Cassy put the Blood Stone back into her pocket then looked back at Keira. "Do you think I can really do this? Can I live up to everything I'm supposed to do?"

"I have faith in you, Cassandra. You just need to have as much confidence in yourself as Frair does."

Cassy knew she was right. She then said a silent prayer she would not betray his faith in her.

"Oh yes, once you return to your realm, the book you were reading will appear as the book Abigail's grandfather brought her all those years ago containing the Blood Key. Of course, it will only be a false vision. For no one but Abigail must ever know what happened here. I have explained everything to Aaron in a dream. I have also cast a spell on him to prevent him from sharing the tale of the two of you coming to Walandra. If knowledge of your travels between the two realms ever reached those who would do you harm, it would be dangerous not only for you but for Aaron as well. Do you understand?"

Cassy nodded her understanding.

"Good. We are done here. It has been an honor, and I know we will see each other again."

Keira reached out and gently touched Cassy on the cheek, then in a flash of light, she was gone.

***

"Cassy, are you alright," Aaron tugged on her hand. "Man, you spaced out."

Frair leaned close to her and whispered in her ear. "Are you sure you're alright. You look pale. Do you need to sit for a moment?"

"No, I'm fine, really. Let's just get this over with."

Cassy grabbed Aaron's hand and tightly held it in hers. "I want to thank all of you for your love and support. I will never forget you."

She then turned and looked at Frair. "I leave my heart with you. I love you, and I always will."

Before Frair could respond, Cassy gently squeezed the Blood Stone, and in a bright flash of light, both she and Aaron vanished.

Chapter 27

"What are you two doing here?" Melissa said as she walked into their great-grandmother's library.

Cassy opened her eyes and saw Melissa glaring down with her hands on her hips. She then lifted her head and looked over at Aaron, who was stirring awake.

"We couldn't sleep, so we came down here to read," Cassy yawned as she sat up in the large over-stuffed chair.

Melissa reached down and flipped the book closed on Cassy's lap. "I thought great-grandmother forbid us from touching this book."

"Huh?" Cassy looked down at the book lying on her lap and realized it was the book from the glass case.

"You're gonna be in so much trouble," Melissa laughed in a low and devious tone.

Cassy quickly jumped to her feet and returned the book to the glass case. "There, no harm is done. She never needs to know."

Melissa walked over to the glass case and ran her finger along the edge.

"True, she doesn't need to know, but wouldn't it be wrong to keep something like this from her?"

Cassy looked at Melissa with fear and shame in her eyes.

"Come on, Melissa. Stop being so mean to her. Neither one of us said anything when you took Mom's car for a late-night drive with your friends last month, did we?"

Melissa looked at Aaron with a surprised expression on her face. "How do you know about that?"

"Come on, Sis, you may have Mom and Dad convinced you're sweet and innocent, but Cassy and I know better," Aaron grinned as he glanced over at Cassy, who was also surprised by this announcement.

"Yeah, how do you think Mom would feel about learning her sweet, little girl stole her car to go on a joyride with her friends?"

Cassy fought to control her joy at seeing Melissa put in her place for a change. Even though Cassy loved her twin sister, she was tired of her always getting away with things because their parents were convinced, she was the perfect daughter.

Melissa realized she was in no place to push her luck. "Fine, I won't say anything, but you better hope she doesn't find out," she huffed, turning on her heel, and then she left the room.

Once Cassy and Aaron were convinced she was gone, they looked at each other and exhaled.

"Dang, that was close," Aaron rolled his eyes.

"Yeah, it was. Hey, how did you know she took Mom's car?"

Aaron looked at Cassy and smiled. "You'd be surprised what I know."

"Dang, remind me never to get on your bad side," Cassy punched him lightly on the shoulder.

"Cassy."

"Yeah," she turned to look at Aaron and noticed the sadness on his face.

"Is it wrong to wish we didn't have to leave?"

Cassy was not sure how to answer his question. While she knew they had to come back, a part of her wanted to stay in Walandra with Frair forever.

"No, it's not wrong, but we both know we needed to come home."

Aaron looked at her and shook his head. "I guess so. I just don't think it will be as exciting hanging with my lame friends when I could be soaring through the clouds with a Dragon. You have to admit Frair is the coolest friend ever."

Cassy felt tears stinging her eyes. "Yes, he is special, isn't he?"

"Cassy, I'm sorry, I shouldn't have..."

"Hey, don't worry. I just need to realize it will never be. I need to put my feelings for him behind me and move on," she reached up and wiped the tears from her eyes. "Come on, my little warrior. Let's get upstairs before anyone else wakes up."

***

Cassy walked over to the bedside table and opened the small drawer. She then reached into the pocket of her robe and pulled out the Blood Stone. She held it up and carefully looked at it.

"So, this is great-grandmother's way back to Roupert? I know he will be thrilled to have her back with him." She gently rubbed her thumb across the face of the Blood Stone, feeling a warm sensation move through her body, reminding her of the link she shared with the Dragons.

"Stop it," she said as she put the Blood Stone in the draw. "I'll give it to Great-grandmother, and that will be it."

The sun peeked through the curtains, letting Cassy know the house would soon be alive with the sounds of the service staff going about their morning duties.

She decided to just sit in the chair by the large window overlooking the ocean and think for a while. As she rested her head on the soft cloth, her mind wandered back to Walandra and Frair.

"How am I going to forget you, Frair?" She whispered as a vision of his smiling face appeared in her mind. She reached for the amulet and held it in her hand, gently rubbing her thumb over its smooth surface.

"I am with you, Cassy. You are never alone," his voice whispered in her mind.

She brought the amulet up to her lips and tenderly kissed it, feeling his love consume her. "Oh, Frair, I miss you already. How am I going to return to my old life after my time with you in Walandra?"

"You are strong, Cassy, much stronger than you realize. You have important things to do, and

I know you will fulfill each task without question. I love you and await the day when we are together again," his voice faded from her mind, leaving her to her own thoughts.

She knew he was right. Keira had given her an important task to do. As to anything else expected of her, only time would tell.

Silence filled her mind when she heard a soft tapping at the door. "Cassy, are you awake? May I come in?" Abigail slowly opened the door and looked toward the bed.

"Sure, Queen Abigail, I'm already awake and enjoying the view of the ocean before breakfast."

Abigail stepped into the room and closed the door behind her. "Thank you, my sweet Princess," Abigail laughed softly as she walked to an empty chair sitting by the window.

"What has you awake so early this morning?" Abigail asked as she took a seat.

Cassy looked at Abigail, and she could see the love in her eyes. "I couldn't sleep. I just had a lot on my mind."

Abigail nodded her head and smiled. "How funny, I had a difficult time sleeping as well. I must admit I had the strangest dream."

Cassy looked at Abigail, curious as to what type of dream would have kept her awake.

"In my dream, I had someone named Keira come to me. She said I was to talk to you in private because you had an urgent message for me. Strange, isn't it?" Abigail shook her head.

Cassy looked at her great-grandmother and realized how much she had given up in her life.

To have the Blood Key take you from the one you love deeply and have the memory stripped from your mind was too horrible to imagine. Nearly as bad as having the memory of a lost love consuming your every thought.

"No, it's not strange at all, In fact, I do have a message for you." Cassy held her breath as she saw the look on Abigail's face transform from one of confusion to one of understanding.

"All these years, I thought it was a dream. I believed it to be the mindless rambling of a foolish girl." Abigail reached up and wiped a tear from her eye.

"Stay here, I have something for you." Cassy stood and walked over to the bedside table, where she had hidden the Blood Stone.

Abigail watched as Cassy pulled something out of the drawer then return to the chair, holding it in her hand.

"What is that?" Abigail asked as she felt excitement stirring up from deep inside of her.

Cassy held out her hand.

"Oh, my, that's the stone from my Grandfather's book. Why did you take it?" Abigail felt her heartbreak at realizing Cassy had disregarded her wishes to leave the book alone.

"Please give me your hand," Cassy asked.

Abigail looked at Cassy, wondering why the strange request. Deciding to see what Cassy would do, she held out her open hand.

"This will answer all of your questions." Cassy placed the stone in the palm of Abigail's outstretched hand.

Abigail felt a strange and familiar sensation consume her. She looked at the stone, which now glowed and vibrated in her hand. "Oh, my, it's the Blood Key! I remember. I remember everything," Abigail cried out with joy.

Cassy watched as Abigail held the Blood Stone to her heart and cried. She then found herself thinking of Frair and wanting to share this moment with him.

"How did you know? I don't understand any of this," Abigail said through tears of pure joy.

"I know because Aaron and I just returned from Walandra."

Surprise filled Abigail at hearing Cassy's confession. "How is that possible, unless…"

"The Blood Key chose me as the new Champion. It took Aaron and me to Walandra, where I was forced to face the Evil Queen Alona." As Cassy said the words, she could barely believe them herself. She knew she would laugh at the story had she not lived through it.

"You've returned. Does Alona still rule?" Abigail held her breath and awaited the answer.

"No, she is banished to the Land of Shadows. All is as it should be in the kingdom. Even King Ashlym has returned to rule with Queen Privlana."

"So, you were able to complete your quest? How wonderful, did anyone help you?" A look of sadness suddenly filled her eyes as she struggled at how to ask the question burning in her mind.

"Yes, the three Lillients helped me, Othan, Frair, and…. Roupert," Cassy waited for the question she knew would inevitably come.

"How are our little friends, Arianna, Syrea, and Brianna doing?" Abigail smiled at the memories of the three little fairies.

"They are doing well. I don't think I could have done it without their help," Cassy grinned, waiting for Abigail to ask of Roupert.

"You said Frair helped you? I was wondering when he would emerge from the egg. I bet he's a wonderful young man."

Cassy fought back her tears, not wanting Abigail to know how she felt about Frair. "Yes, he was wonderful. At first, I thought of him as a silly, little Dragon, but once Queen Privlana's spell was broken, I realized what an exceptional person he really is."

Abigail watched as Cassy spoke of Frair, and she could not help but notice a hint of sadness and longing in her voice. She looked carefully at Cassy and saw the emotions playing out on her face. It was then that she knew. "You're in love with Frair, aren't you?"

Cassy sat in stunned silence, not sure of how to respond.

"Does he return your feelings for him?" Abigail looked deeply into Cassy's eyes.

Cassy turned her face away and looked out of the window, searching for the best words to respond.

Abigail gasped as her hand covered her mouth. "Oh, my, you do understand what it means when a Dragon gives their heart in love, don't you?"

Cassy nodded her head, not wanting to meet Abigail's gaze. "Yes, I understand."

Cassy rested her hand on the amulet, hidden beneath her pajama top, feeling the warm sensation caressing her.

"I don't understand. You banished the Evil Queen, fell in love with Prince Frair, had the chance to live a life that most would only dream of, and yet, you still came back? Why?"

Cassy turned and looked at Abigail, unsure of how to answer the question. She knew what she wanted to say but thought better of it. "I had to come back. I needed to bring Aaron home, and I promised to bring you the Blood Stone."

Abigail shook her head in disbelief. "I can understand bringing Aaron home, but why leave just to bring the Blood Stone to an old woman who is in her final days of life. My dear, you have your entire life ahead of you. You have a Dragon, who has given you his heart, and that is something special. If I had the chance to be with my true love, I would go without a second thought."

"But you do have the opportunity to be with your true love. In fact, he waits for you in Walandra," Cassy said with a smile. "Why haven't you asked of him yet?"

Abigail looked at Cassy, surprised by this statement. "Are you speaking of Roupert?"

Cassy nodded her head.

"Are you saying Roupert remembers me after all of these years? How is that possible? I was sure he had moved on with his life."

"How could he move on with his life when you possessed his heart?" Cassy smiled when she saw the look of joy appear on Abigail's face.

"I just assumed..." she wiped tears from her eyes.

"I had to come back to bring you the Blood Stone so you could return to Walandra. Keira said you would know the proper time as the Blood Stone would let you know. Roupert is a wonderful man, so I can see why you love him. I'm sorry you have spent all of these years alone," Cassy brushed her hand across the amulet again feeling the same soothing warmth emanating from it.

Abigail leaned forward and hugged Cassy tightly. "Thank you. I can't begin to tell you how happy this makes me. I would often dream of Roupert and Walandra, but once I awoke, I believed it to all be the longing of a lonely, old woman."

Cassy rested her head on Abigail's shoulder. She was glad to have given her great-grandmother hope for the future, but a small corner of her heart ached for her own loss.

Abigail stood and took Cassy by the hand. "Come on, my dear. I smell our breakfast, and we want to get there before your little brother eats it all."

Both women laughed then headed to the dining room.

Chapter 28

The rest of the week went uneventfully. Cassy and Abigail had spent hours talking. Abigail shared stories of her life, as well as her time as the Champion in Walandra. Cassy enjoyed this opportunity to get to know her great-grandmother better, and when the time to go home arrived, she found herself sad to leave. Melissa, on the other hand, was thrilled to be going home.

"I can't wait to get home. I cannot believe she didn't have any television or internet. How is that even possible today? She's nice, but a week was too long," Melissa groaned as she shoved her last pair of shorts into her suitcase.

"Maybe you would have had a better time if you weren't just sitting around and doing your nails all the time. Sheez, Melissa, there's more to life than getting a mani-pedi."

Melissa looked at Cassy and rolled her eyes. "Not everyone strives to be a social zero. I have an image I must protect, even if you don't."

Realizing she might as well be talking to the wall, Cassy decided to leave Melissa to finish her packing. Before she had gone to Walandra and faced everything there, Cassy would have argued to make her point with Melissa. Yet, now she realized there was no point in fighting. "Okay, I'll see you downstairs."

As Cassy walked toward the door, Melissa looked at her and shook her head when she realized there was something different about her sister. "Thanks. Do you need any help packing?"

"No, mine is already done and downstairs by the front door," Cassy smiled as she walked out into the hallway and went down the staircase.

"Hey Cassy, we're in here," Aaron shouted from the library.

Cassy walked into the library and found Aaron and Abigail sitting at the reading table with a stack of books sitting in front of them.

"What are you two up to?" Cassy laughed when she saw the looks on their faces.

"Queen Abigail said I can take any of these books home with me." He pointed excitedly to the stack of books.

"Oh, my, so you're planning to read all of those?"

"I sure am. She told me there are adventures of knights, dragons, and magic in these. I told her those were some of my favorite things. Isn't she cool?" Aaron grinned as he leaned his head on her shoulder.

"Well, we better get those packed in something for the trip." Cassy looked around the room, hoping to find something to use.

"Don't worry, my dear, Mr. Saunders has gone to get a case to pack these in as we speak," Abigail chuckled when she saw the excited look on Aaron's face.

Mr. Saunders walked through the door carrying a large leather case. He then set it on the table next to the books and began packing them inside.

Abigail stood and looked at Aaron and Cassy. "Come, let's go wait out on the porch. It's a lovely day, so it's a shame to waste it by staying inside."

Aaron jumped to his feet, "I'll race you outside."

"Oh, no, you don't," Cassy laughed as they both rushed to the door with Abigail following them.

***

The long black limousine pulled up in front of the house and stopped. Mr. Saunders stepped outside, pulling a small cart with the suitcases and the leather case filled with Aaron's books.

Aaron jumped to his feet. "Do you need any help?"

"Thank you, but no. Please sit until it's time to leave," Mr. Saunders said flatly.

Cassy and Abigail exchanged amused glances as they watched a disappointed Aaron return to his seat.

"Don't feel bad, Aaron. He's grumpy with me as well," Abigail grinned when she saw the surprised look on Aaron's face.

Once Mr. Sanders had the luggage in the trunk, he waved for the children to join him. "You will need to let Miss Melissa know it's time to leave."

"I'll get her." Aaron jumped to his feet and went inside of the house.

"Well, I guess it's time for you to go. I'm going to miss you terribly," Abigail said with tears filling her eyes.

"I'm going to miss you, too. You'll let me know before you return to Walandra, won't you?"

Abigail reached into her pocket and pulled out the Blood Stone. "As soon as this tells me it's time, I'll let you know."

"Gosh, Aaron, I was on the phone with Jennifer. You don't have to be so rude," Melissa huffed as she followed Aaron outside.

"Hey, I told you it was time to go. It's not my fault you kept talking," Aaron teased.

"You just wait until we get home and I tell Mom about what a brat you are," Melissa groaned as she walked down the steps to the waiting limousine.

"Dang Melissa, you're the one who's being rude," Cassy said as she followed Aaron down the steps to the limousine.

Mr. Saunders held the door open, allowing Melissa to get inside and sit on the other side next to the window. Aaron stopped before getting in and then waited for Abigail to join them.

"Thank you for letting us come for a visit. I love you, and I hope we get to come back soon," tears filled his eyes as he hugged her tightly.

Abigail held him close. "I love you, too, and I hope you come and see me again soon."

Aaron jumped into the limousine and sat across from Melissa, making her complain when he accidentally kicked her foot.

"Ouch, watch where you put those huge feet of yours."

Aaron laughed when he saw the look of disgust on her face. "Hey, maybe it's your feet that are the big ones."

"I can't wait to get home so I can get the heck away from you." Melissa crossed her hands over her chest and glared out of the window.

"Ma'am, we need to get going. The pilot is scheduled to leave in thirty minutes," Mr. Saunders announced in a firm voice.

Cassy looked at Abigail and smiled. "Well, I guess it's time to go. I'm going to miss you, Queen Abigail. I hope you don't mind if I call you from time to time?"

"Oh, that would be lovely. I miss you already," she grabbed Cassy and held her close.

Cassy pressed her cheek to Abigail's cheek and whispered in her ear, "If you need me, I promise to be there for you. I love you."

Abigail pulled Cassy closer. "I love you, too. Thank you for everything."

Mr. Saunders cleared his throat. "Ladies, we must get going."

Abigail released Cassy after giving her a kiss on the forehead. "Give your Mother and Father my love, will you?"

"I will," Cassy then climbed into the back of the limousine.

Abigail leaned down and looked in the back seat. "Goodbye, Princess Melissa."

Melissa turned and looked at Abigail with a look of embarrassment on her face for her previous behavior. She knew she had acted horribly. It's just the last few days Melissa had felt like an outsider. Ever since the night she had found Cassy and Aaron in the library, she didn't seem to be a part of the group.

"Goodbye, Queen Abigail. Thank you for a fun visit." Melissa forced a smile, and then she turned her face back toward the window.

Abigail gave the three of them a playful wink. "I look forward to our next visit."

Mr. Saunders closed the door before he climbed into the driver's seat. After turning on the ignition, he put the car in gear.

Cassy looked out of the back window and watched the lone figure of Abigail fade away as they drove down the long driveway toward the private airport with the airplane that would take them back to their lives.

Eleven Months Later

Swirling smoke filled the nostrils of those trapped in the Land of the Shadows with the pungent order of sulfur. Every creature lived in terror, cursing the day of their banishment into the darkness forever. All did their best to remain unseen, all except for one.

"Do not tell me I cannot leave. I have gathered all the Demlins under my control, and my power is stronger now than ever. No foolish Champion is going to keep me from my goal. I was weak, but now no force can stop me. No

Champion, no Dragons. I will rule unbound from the limitations of my fleshly body. I am no longer Queen Alona. I am now the Dark Queen of Death, and all those who stood against me will suffer. Be they in Walandra or the realm of the Champion...

Please take a moment to leave a review

I invite you to join Cassy on a new adventure as she once again battles

the evil forces in

Return to Walandra

Book 2

The Legend of the Dragon's Blood Key